Books by Shirleen Davies

Historical Western Romance Series
MacLarens of Fire Mountain

Tougher than the Rest, Book One
Faster than the Rest, Book Two
Harder than the Rest, Book Three
Stronger than the Rest, Book Four
Deadlier than the Rest, Book Five
Wilder than the Rest, Book Six

Redemption Mountain

Redemption's Edge, Book One
Wildfire Creek, Book Two
Sunrise Ridge, Book Three
Dixie Moon, Book Four
Survivor Pass, Book Five
Promise Trail, Book Six
Deep River, Book Seven
Courage Canyon, Book Eight
Forsaken Falls, Book Nine
Solitude Gorge, Book Ten
Rogue Rapids, Book Eleven, Coming next in the series!

MacLarens of Boundary Mountain

Colin's Quest, Book One,
Brodie's Gamble, Book Two

Quinn's Honor, Book Three
Sam's Legacy, Book Four
Heather's Choice, Book Five
Nate's Destiny, Book Six
Blaine's Wager, Book Seven, Coming next in the
series!

Contemporary Romance Series

MacLarens of Fire Mountain

Second Summer, Book One
Hard Landing, Book Two
One More Day, Book Three
All Your Nights, Book Four
Always Love You, Book Five
Hearts Don't Lie, Book Six
No Getting Over You, Book Seven
'Til the Sun Comes Up, Book Eight
Foolish Heart, Book Nine
Forever Love, Book Ten, Coming next in the
series!

Peregrine Bay

Reclaiming Love, Book One, A Novella
Our Kind of Love, Book Two

Burnt River

Shane's Burden, Book One by Peggy Henderson

Thorn's Journey, Book Two by Shirleen Davies
Aqua's Achilles, Book Three by Kate Cambridge
Ashley's Hope, Book Four by Amelia Adams
Harpur's Secret, Book Five by Kay P. Dawson
Mason's Rescue, Book Six by Peggy L.
Henderson
Del's Choice, Book Seven by Shirleen Davies
Ivy's Search, Book Eight by Kate Cambridge
Phoebe's Fate, Book Nine by Amelia Adams
Brody's Shelter, Book Ten by Kay P. Dawson
Boone's Surrender, Book Eleven by Shirleen
Davies
Watch for more books in the series!

The best way to stay in touch is to subscribe to my newsletter. Go to www.shirleendavies.com and subscribe in the box at the top of the right column that asks for your email. You'll be notified of new books before they are released, have chances to win great prizes, and receive other subscriber-only specials.

Solitude Gorge

Redemption Mountain Historical Western Romance Series

SHIRLEEN DAVIES

Book Ten in the Redemption Mountain

Historical Western Romance Series

ISBN: 978-1-941786-74-1

Description

Solitude Gorge, Book Ten, Redemption Mountain Historical Western Romance Series

Travis Dixon carved out a life in the rugged Montana territory, far away from the memories of a past defined by the Civil War and personal tragedy. Training wild horses fills his days, while bunkhouse chatter completes his nights. An unlikely friendship with a beautiful widow provides the only female companionship he's had since the heartbreaking death of his wife and daughter.

Isabella Boucher, a wealthy East Coast widow, is content working as a nanny to a prominent ranching family. She's developed friendships she can depend upon and a special bond with a man fighting his broken past. A man she loves, but who is unable to return her affection.

Stunned when Travis decides to put distance between them, she makes the difficult decision to accept invitations from other eligible men. In time, she hopes to forget her love for the rugged cowboy and force him from her heart.

Unfortunately, she learns choices such as this
are never that easy. As much as Isabella yearns
for a life with Travis, their tragic histories form a
barrier neither can surmount.

The arrival of a friend from Isabella's past, plus a
series of events threatening the town, forces
them to take a hard look at themselves, at the
same time doing their best to stay out of the
crosshairs of a new enemy.

Danger lurks in every direction, appearing in the
form of men without conscience or remorse.

Will protecting each other help break down their
walls or force another wedge between them?
Will Travis be able to push his pain aside to see
what's been in front of him all along?

Solitude Gorge, book ten in the Redemption
Mountain historical western romance series, is a
full-length novel with an HEA and no
cliffhanger.

**Visit my website for a list of characters
for each series.**
http://www.shirleendavies.com/character-
list.html

Acknowledgements

As always, many thanks to my wonderful husband for reading every chapter as soon as it's written, my editor, Kim Young, proofreader, Alicia Carmical, Joseph Murray, who is superb at formatting my books for print and electronic versions, and my cover designer, Kim Killion.

Solitude Gorge

Prologue

Battle of Yellow Tavern
Virginia, May 1864

Confederate First Lieutenant Travis Dixon sat atop his horse, the rest of the men in J.E.B. Stuart's Army of Northern Virginia surrounding him. All stared at the most powerful cavalry force ever assembled with over ten thousand Union soldiers primed for battle.

Travis didn't have to figure the math to know the North outnumbered the South by at least three divisions and two brigades. In all his time under Stuart's command, he'd never felt the trepidation he did today.

Behind him stood the abandoned stagecoach inn, Yellow Tavern. General Stuart and one of his staff officers rode past it to join the men, surveying the scene. The look on his commander's face told Travis all he needed to know. The normally ebullient general, the man who rallied the gray knights over and over, stared at the massive force mounted against them. At thirty-one, his imposing presence was all most men needed to steel their resolve. One look, and Travis knew today would be different.

Forcing his gaze away from Stuart, Travis watched as battalions of Union horse artillery moved into position. His mind wandered to his wife and daughter, praying for their safety on their Tennessee farm. He sent up a plea if he died this day, they'd go on without him and not despair his loss.

In the next instant, Travis's thoughts shattered when Stuart shouted for his men to dismount, an order seldom heard from the aggressive general.

Doing as his commander instructed, the men slid to the ground, one man holding the reins of four horses as the others brandished sabers and pistols. It wasn't how Travis wanted to face their Northern opponents, but it wasn't his decision to make.

Several hundred yards to their left, a group of over two hundred Union riders, swords drawn, charged straight toward them. They'd just engaged the enemy when, behind them, another Union group joined the cavalry charge. The war cries from the Northern invaders, along with the ear-splitting roar of cannon fire, intensified the already brutal clash of two well-trained armies.

Firing his pistol while wielding his saber, Travis glanced behind him. Stuart rode one direction, then another, brandishing his sword, shouting encouragement. Smoke and screams filled the air. Surviving was all Travis could think about as he and his comrades advanced, then retreated.

Amidst the chaos, the sharp report of a .44 caliber revolver drew his attention. Slicing his saber through the air, he glanced behind him. Stuart's plumed hat fell to the ground, the general clutching his side as he worked to remain atop his mount.

Turning back to his opponents, Travis fired before his panicked gaze sought out Stuart again. This time, the general lay propped against a tree, the fight seeming to seep from him.

Anger gripped Travis. Screaming in rage, he ran forward, cutting the saber through the air while firing his pistol. Charging toward a scrambling group of Union soldiers, he aimed at the largest. He had little chance to enjoy the slight satisfaction of hitting his opponent before a flash of pain drove through his left thigh. As he faltered, the butt of a rifle swung toward him. His futile effort to thwart the blow did nothing.

Crumbling to the ground, his vision blurred with pain, body betraying him. Travis's last thoughts were of his wife and daughter.

"Lieutenant Dixon?"

The soft voice he'd heard in his sleep came again, a hand clasping his arm. He mumbled something unintelligible and tried to open his eyes. They felt heavy, as if a coin sat on each.

"Lieutenant Dixon, can you open your eyes?"

Moving his head to one side, he groaned at the pain. Forcing his eyes open to slits, he saw a woman wearing a dark dress protected by a deeply stained apron. Her hair fell in tendrils along the sides of her face, the bun loosening to tip to one side.

"Where..." He didn't recognize his own raspy voice. Wincing, he tried to sit up, feeling a firm hand pushing him back down. "Where am..."

"A good ways from the battle, I'm afraid. Can you take a sip of water?"

Nodding, he did his best to lift his head, grateful for the support of the woman's hand. After three small sips, she removed the cup, settling his head back on the pillow. As the water refreshed him, it also brought back memories of the fight.

"The other men?" He hissed the words through parched lips.

"A wagon brought you and several men here a few days ago." Her voice was soft, soothing. "No one knows how they made it. Those Yankees took groups of men hostage, marching them away. I wouldn't question too much why you made it here and others didn't."

Squeezing his eyes shut, he thought a moment, before a sharp pain flashed through him. "My leg?" Reaching down, his hand rested on this left thigh.

"You still have it, Lieutenant. The doctor who tended you thought he'd have to amputate. When he checked a few hours later, he changed his mind. You're a lucky man."

Although grateful they'd spared his leg, Travis didn't feel lucky. "I need to get back. The men need me." The determination did nothing to move his weakened body.

She glanced down at him, her smooth features and soft gray eyes meeting his. "As I said, you're a lucky man. When you leave here, you'll be heading home. Many others will not."

Chapter One

Redemption's Edge Ranch
Splendor, Montana Territory
July 1869

Travis Dixon removed his hat, swiping moisture from his forehead. July in Montana could be mild or blistering. One never knew which to expect when stepping outside the bunkhouse door. Today, the sun's relentless heat sent the men to the water bucket several times each hour.

"Are you going to stand there watching me, or are you going to get your own mustang?" The slow upward curve of Wyatt Jackson's mouth belied the mirth behind his sharp question. "We have at least twenty to go before filling the Army contract."

Shaking his head, Travis settled the hat back on his head. Ever since marrying Nora Evans, the sheriff's sister, Wyatt had found peace, putting much of his difficult past behind him.

"You're sure getting bossy since marrying that fine woman. I thought it might mellow you a bit." Grabbing a halter from a hook outside the barn, Travis opened the corral gate, striding past Wyatt.

"That fine woman is why I'm anxious to get home."

Waving a dismissive hand in the air, Travis approached an adjacent corral. The wild horses snorted and pranced, one moving toward him, the rest shifting to the other side of the enclosure.

He knew the exact one he wanted. The horse had taunted him since the first day they'd rounded up the herd a few miles south of the ranch. A stocky buckskin with black mane and tail, the stallion ran back and forth on the other side of the gate, daring Travis to catch him.

Wyatt stepped next to him, crossing his arms. "Are you sure you want to try tackling him right now? He's looking especially ornery today."

Straightening the halter, slipping it up his arm and over his shoulder, Travis's gaze locked on the horse. "No time better than now."

With a flick of his wrist, he opened the gate, slipping into the corral before Wyatt followed, securing the latch behind them. They worked together at a slow pace, encouraging the horse in low voices while using rolled lariats to cut the stallion off from his band of mares and foals.

Twice, Travis thought they had the horse cornered. Each time, he reared back, charging past both men. After half an hour, the stallion moved toward the fence separating the two corrals. Travis backed his way to the gate, throwing it open before Wyatt herded the horse away from his mares and through the opening.

The mustang stomped his hooves, snorted, then took off to the other side of the corral. They continued to press him, not letting the stallion rest. He had the run of a large fenced area and used every square foot. Another half an hour passed before the horse tired enough for Travis to get a noose around his neck. A moment later, Wyatt did the same with his rope, prompting another round of bucking. The stallion refused to yield.

Arms burning, the men struggled to keep a tight hold on the large beast. Snorting and bucking, he tested their limits, taunting them with his renewed determination to get away. He didn't realize Travis and Wyatt had no intention of giving up.

Then everything stopped. The stallion came to a halt, chest heaving, nostrils flaring. Never taking his gaze from the animal, Travis moved until he stood a foot away, close enough to reach out and stroke the mustang's neck. He continued the motions, talking in a soothing voice as Wyatt closed the distance between him and the animal.

With both men stroking his neck, whispering encouragement, the stallion's fight slowly dissolved. Using the other end of his rope, Travis rubbed it over the horse's nose, letting the animal get used to the feel. After several minutes, he let the halter slip off his shoulder, replacing the rope as he continued to stroke the stallion's neck.

Keeping their ropes in place, Wyatt continued the tension as Travis edged the halter over the animal's nose and into place. Attaching the lead rope to the halter, both men let the nooses fall away.

Travis and the stallion were on their own as Wyatt stepped back, moving to the edge of the fence.

Removing his hat, Wyatt wiped away the sweat. "I do believe that's the orneriest horse I've ever worked. You want to try saddling him today?"

Travis shook his head. "I'm whipped." He blew out a breath as the stallion tried to create more distance between them. "My arms are ready to fall off. I'll walk him around a bit and start again tomorrow."

Wyatt watched his friend guide the horse in circles before removing the lead rope, keeping the halter in place. Walking away, Travis glanced over his shoulder a couple times before joining Wyatt at the fence.

"Hardest stallion I've ever worked. I don't know about you, but I need water." Opening the gate, Travis's gaze focused on a buggy coming toward them...and the woman driving it.

Wyatt looked at him, lifting a brow. "Looks like your lady friend has come for a visit."

My lady friend.

Travis let out a breath, knowing he felt much more for Isabella Boucher than just a friend. In the time they'd known each other, shared confidences and became close, he'd never been able to express his feelings. Worse, he didn't know if he'd ever be able to go beyond a close friendship.

Clasping him on the shoulder, Wyatt lowered his voice. "Are you ever going to tell her what's going on in your head?"

Glancing at the ground, Travis shook his head. "I've got to understand it myself before saying anything to her."

"She won't wait forever."

Travis's jaw worked, but all he could offer was a curt nod before walking toward the buggy.

"Good afternoon, Isabella." Lifting his arms, he placed them around her waist, lowering her to the ground. "I didn't know you were coming out today."

Taking off her gloves, she folded them carefully, taking her time, then slipped them into her reticule. Reaching up, she adjusted her hat before letting her gaze meet his, clutching her hands in front of her.

"I've not seen you since Wyatt and Nora married. Not even at church."

He felt the guilt build. They'd always met each other before church, sat together, then talked for a while after the service. Most times, they'd have supper with the sheriff, Gabe Evans, his wife, Lena, and their son, Jack. Lena and Isabella had been friends since childhood. At one time, Isabella had been Jack's guardian, taking care of him while Lena sorted out some difficult issues in her life. Travis had always enjoyed their meals with the Evans family.

Lately, for reasons he couldn't explain, he'd felt the need to put distance between him and Isabella. Instead of being honest with her, he'd stayed away from town on Sundays, choosing to work with the horses. Travis rationalized his actions, telling himself they had horses to break, Army contracts to fill.

He crossed his arms, staring at his boots before lifting his gaze to hers. "I've been working long hours, trying to catch up after the fire. There's been much to do."

She stared at him, her features impassive. "I see." Isabella glanced at the porch, seeing no one had yet come out to greet her. "It's strange, though. You've never had a problem riding over to Luke's to visit me before. Even after the fire, no more than two days went by before you came to see me."

Travis had no good answer. How did you tell the woman you cared so deeply about you weren't ready to begin again?

The death of his wife and daughter tore his world apart, created a void no one had been able to fill until he'd met Isabella. Even so, he'd never been able to speak the words or tell her of his inability to commit. Travis didn't believe he ever could.

"Well, I suppose—" He stopped at the sound of voices on the porch.

"Isabella! I didn't know you were coming out this evening. You'll stay for supper and the night, won't you?" Rachel, Dax Pelletier's wife, walked down the steps. Behind her, Ginny, Luke Pelletier's wife, followed behind, carrying their young son, Cooper.

Returning her friends' hugs, Isabella stepped back. "I only planned to come by to speak with Travis." She shot him a mild glance.

He touched the brim of his hat. "If you ladies will excuse me..." His eyes locked on Isabella for an extended moment before he turned and walked away.

Isabella's face fell, her heart cracking.

"Are you all right?" Rachel placed a hand on her friend's arm, her eyes full of concern.

Swallowing a hard knot of disappointment, she nodded. "I will be."

"Is something wrong between you and Travis?" Ginny settled Cooper on a hip, her gaze following him as he disappeared into the barn.

Letting out a breath, Isabella couldn't help the sadness washing over her. She'd given him time to reconcile his past, been a friend, provided support and encouragement. Every time he looked at her, she felt the love, yet he'd never spoken the words. Not hearing from him in weeks, coupled with his response today, provided all she needed to know.

"No, Ginny. Travis and I are fine. The same as always...just friends." Shooting one more quick look at the barn, she turned back to her friends. "Did you say there's enough food for me to join you for supper?"

Slipping an arm through Isabella's, Rachel nodded. "More than enough. And an extra bedroom so you don't have to drive back tonight."

Isabella lived with Luke and Ginny at their ranch house a few miles away. She'd been with them during Ginny's pregnancy and Cooper's birth, acting somewhat as a nanny. Many days, Luke brought Ginny and Cooper to the main ranch house, allowing them to spend time with Rachel and her two sons, Patrick and James.

Stepping inside the house, the full impact of Travis's actions, or lack thereof, hit her. She'd been in love with him from almost the first day they'd met. Her husband had recently passed away, sparking her decision to come west with Lena's son, Jack. Travis provided companionship, someone to share her hopes and burdens. He'd shared the terrible tragedy of finding his wife and daughter had died while he served in the Confederate cavalry.

Travis had fought for the South. Her sentiments slanted to the North. Still, they'd found a way to bridge the gap, becoming close, although never lovers. She now had to accept they'd never be more than what they were today. He'd given all he could.

On a shaky sigh, Isabella accepted the fact she needed more.

Travis rested his arms on the top rail of the fence, watching the stallion prance about, shaking his head and snorting. The horse had given them quite a fight, and he still had more left inside him. Travis didn't doubt the ride to tame the horse would be wild and rocky.

"Coffee?" Dirk Masters, one of two ranch foremen, joined him at the fence, holding out a steaming cup.

Accepting it, Travis nodded. "Thanks."

Dirk stared at the stallion, seeing him move close, then dash away when either he or Travis shifted. "It surprised me to see you here. I thought you'd have supper inside the big house with Isabella." Dirk and his wife, Rosemary, lived in a small house not far from the larger Pelletier home.

Blowing across the top of the coffee, Travis took a sip. "Not tonight."

Dirk didn't respond right away. "It must be hard for both of you. Having been married and losing everything. I can't imagine life without Rosemary."

Chuckling, Travis glanced at his friend. "It wasn't long ago you two couldn't stand the sight of each other."

Dirk shrugged, tipping back his cup to finish his coffee. "Can't explain it myself. I guess you just know when it's right."

"Rosemary's a handful."

Nodding, Dirk tapped the cup against the fence, dislodging a few leftover coffee grounds. "That she is. But she says the same of me. Now, Isabella's quiet, refined. I don't believe I've ever heard her raise her voice. I doubt she has a mean bone in her body."

"I can't disagree." Travis didn't want to talk about Isabella. "Wyatt is staying in town tomorrow to work on the house they're renting from Gabe and Lena. If you're going to be around, I'd appreciate help with the stallion."

Dirk snorted. "He's a nasty one. Is he part of the Army contract?"

"Not this one. Dax and Luke want to put him to stud. I can't say as I blame them. He's smart, his lines are good, and he's strong."

Staring into the corral, Dirk watched the stallion continue to paw at the ground. "It's his attitude I wonder about."

"We plan to have him breed with Lydia's mare, Angel."

Dirk's eyes widened. "That sweet thing? What does Bull say?"

Bull Mason was the other foreman at Redemption's Edge. He'd married Lydia, one of the ranch orphans, and they now had a son. He was known to be exceedingly protective of his family and friends.

"He trusts Dax and Luke. Lydia was the one they had to convince. I do believe she's softened."

"You know, Isabella doesn't have a horse. I'm thinking you should train one for her. Maybe a mare like Angel, or Nora's horse, Sugar. It'd be a nice gift."

Rubbing his chin, he winced, acknowledging how he'd never once given Isabella a present. Other than sharing a meal in town a few times, he'd never given her any token of his affection.

Thinking back, he recalled all the times he'd walked into the family home in Tennessee with a small bouquet of wild flowers or a length of ribbon from town for his wife. His throat constricted at the thought and the pain that always followed.

The fever had spread through their small town with a vengeance few had ever seen. Some families were spared, others wiped out. According to his neighbors, his wife had kept their daughter isolated while she tended to the sick. When it appeared the death toll had peaked, his wife came down with the fever, followed by his daughter soon afterward. No matter what their neighbors did to stop the illness, neither lasted more than a few days.

It seemed cruel to survive the ravages of the war only to be brought down by fever, dysentery, or consumption. No one was immune from loss.

Falling in love with another woman and marrying a second time held little appeal. Even if he changed his mind someday, he'd never have more children. Losing his wife had broken

Travis's heart. The death of his daughter had devastated him. He'd never choose to go through such crushing pain again.

"Isabella would want children." Travis winced at his whispered words. He rarely shared any thoughts on his past or future. He felt Dirk's gaze on him.

Dirk shifted his feet, looking back at the stallion. "And you don't." It wasn't a question. He knew how Travis lost his family.

Giving a brief shake of his head, Travis stared past the corral at nothing in particular. "Isabella's good with children. She deserves a whole passel of them."

"Does she know how you feel?"

Another wave of guilt washed over him. No matter how much he cared for Isabella, he didn't have it in him to commit again, face the uncertainty of a future that brought little except hard work and death.

"I've been thinking of telling her."

Stepping away from the fence, Dirk looked over his shoulder at the big house, hearing voices waft through the open windows.

"You need to be honest with her, Travis. She's too fine a woman to be left hanging on to hope for something that'll never be. Before you do, make damn certain it's what you want. Once you have the conversation, you may never be able to take the words back." He clasped Travis on the shoulder before strolling away, his steps slow and precise.

Watching him leave, a deep sorrow ripped through Travis, one having nothing to do with the loss of his family. Isabella had been a friend when he most needed one. She always brought sunshine to his dark life, peace to his battered soul. He didn't want to give those up, but he knew the time had come for him to toss aside his selfish motives and think of the beautiful woman who meant so much to him.

The thought of being open with her sickened him. The thought of keeping her from having a future with a man who could give her everything made him feel small and cowardly.

Letting out a breath, he took one last look at the stallion before turning toward the bunkhouse. He'd speak with her before she left in the morning. It was a bittersweet decision, providing Travis with no relief and a bleak future.

Chapter Two

Splendor

Isabella stared onto the street through the window of the restaurant in Suzanne's boardinghouse, her cup of coffee long since cold and unappetizing. It had been almost a week since she'd gone to see Travis, but the pain of his words as she climbed onto the buggy hadn't lessened.

A part of her knew to be prepared for bad news. The shock of hearing Travis confess he'd never be able to give her more than what they already had still crushed her. Isabella hadn't known the depth of her feelings until he'd dashed them, setting her free to find someone else.

Cradling the cup with both hands, she squeezed, having the strangest desire to see the china shatter, the same as Travis had done to her heart. He hoped they could continue as friends, occasionally still sitting together at church. She'd responded with a curt nod, unable to get her voice to work. When he'd tried once more to explain, she'd slapped the lines, getting the buggy moving to put as much distance between them as possible. It had been rude and completely unlike her. Still, she couldn't find it in her to feel the least bit regretful at leaving him slack-jawed, staring after her.

"More coffee?"

Shifting her attention to the woman standing next to her, Isabella shook her head. "No, thank you, Suzanne. Two cups are more than enough."

Taking a seat next to her, Suzanne set the pot down. "Are you doing all right? You don't seem yourself today."

She thought of telling her friend she was fine. Instead, she stared down at her cup, shaking her head. "I rode out to see Travis a few days ago. He, um...he told me I'm free to find someone else."

Suzanne's eyes widened. "Travis Dixon said that to you? Why, he has less brains than the donkey Noah keeps at the livery."

Despite the hurt she felt, Isabella's mouth curved into a grim smile. "Much less."

"What did you say to him?"

Isabella's gaze met hers. "Nothing. It shocked me so much, I couldn't speak. Couldn't even form a coherent thought. I was already in the buggy, so I slapped the lines and left." Shifting to look back outside, she shrugged. "Besides, there's not much you can do when someone doesn't love you. Any reply would've sounded angry and bitter."

"I'm sure you felt both." Suzanne placed a hand on her arm. "Any woman would with the length of time he's been courting you."

Letting out a shaky breath, Isabella bit her lower lip. "I don't believe Travis ever saw our relationship as courting. In his mind, we were good friends, nothing more."

"Although you wanted more."

Isabella gave a slow nod. "I was so certain he cared for me."

"Don't fool yourself, honey. Travis loves you."

A notch appeared between her brows. "How can you even think that after what I've told you?"

Suzanne sat back, smirking. "It's all over his face every time you're together. Why, most everyone expected him to marry you."

Groaning, Isabella felt her body go cold. "Then everyone would be wrong. It seems marriage is the furthest thing from his mind. He did tell me he never wanted more children and knew I dreamed of a large family. I believe it was his way of making his decision sound more rational and less emotional. Instead, it made me feel worse."

Suzanne tilted her head to the side. "I don't understand."

Isabella's face pinched. "If I didn't want children, perhaps he could've seen me differently. Perhaps even fallen in love with me."

"Now that is the silliest thing I've ever heard you say. Sounds to me like Travis is making excuses for his inability to commit to marriage.

The little I know of his late wife and daughter, it makes sense he'd be real cautious about starting another family. It doesn't stop me from wanting to slap some sense into him." Standing, Suzanne lifted a hand when Isabella started to do the same. "You stay right here. There's just one cure for this and I happen to have it in my kitchen."

An amused expression crossed Isabella's face. Besides time, she knew of no cure for what she felt. A moment later, she broke into a full smile.

"Misery is meant to be shared." Suzanne set down two plates, each holding a large slice of chocolate cake. Pulling a clean cup from her apron, she sat down, filling it with coffee. Picking up her fork, she looked at Isabella. "This is a time-proven way to get over a broken heart."

Taking a huge bite, Isabella chewed, her eyes closing as she savored the rare treat. Swallowing, she glanced at Suzanne. "Wherever did you get chocolate?"

"Baron Klaussner brought it with him from New York. He said no menu is complete without chocolate cake."

Everyone in Splendor had been shocked when Baron Ernst Wolfgang Klaussner and his son, Johann, arrived from New York with a full entourage. Although somewhat hesitant to accept him, he'd proven to be as genial as he was strict and proper.

Taking another bite, Isabella smiled. "I do believe the baron is right. How much cake is left?"

Suzanne laughed. "Enough to cure several broken hearts. Do you want another slice?"

She glanced at her empty plate. "Absolutely."

Redemption's Edge

"Two more and we'll have what we need for the contract." Travis studied the remaining mares. He and Wyatt had left what they considered the easiest horses for last. Watching Wyatt walk into the corral toward a horse already bucking, snorting, and pawing at the ground, Travis hoped they'd made the right decision.

He felt fortunate for the heavy workload over the last week. Up at dawn, falling onto his bunk late at night, exhausted from the grueling pace of breaking the wild horses. As much as he'd hoped the fatigue would keep his mind off Isabella, it hadn't. A week after seeing her, he still found himself staring at the ceiling, unable to sleep until a few hours before sunup. His mind told him he'd been wise to push Isabella away. His heart had a different response. Travis couldn't stop wondering if he'd made a huge mistake, one he'd never be able to correct.

"I've got several of the men saddling up to ride toward the gorge. That's the last place we spotted the other herd." Dirk stopped next to Travis, his gaze locked on Wyatt.

Giving himself a mental shake, Travis shoved thoughts of Isabella out of his head. "Do you want me to go with them?"

"Does Wyatt need you here to finish with the last two mares?"

Travis's eyes crinkled as he watched his friend work his magic on the skittish horse. "You'll need one man to keep watch in case anything happens."

Dirk nodded. "I'll send Billy over while you join the others. Mal and Tat are in the group riding out with you."

At eighteen, Billy Zales had come a long way since he and several other orphans were discovered living in a cave near the ranch. Like Wyatt and Travis, Billy had a talent for breaking and training horses.

Dirk took off in one direction while Travis headed toward a nearby corral, whistling for Banjo, his large sorrel gelding.

After his injury at the Battle of Yellow Tavern, he'd never recovered his horse, believing the Union cavalry confiscated him along with many others. He'd been lucky to barter Banjo from a neighbor who'd stayed with Travis's wife and daughter until there was nothing more anyone could do. The man had been happy to give Travis the gelding in exchange for two cows. Another neighbor bought his property at a fair price, more than Travis expected.

Banjo was one of only two tangible ties to his past. The other, a frayed and wrinkled image of his wife, daughter, and him taken days before he left for the war. He kept it tucked into a Bible, looking at it every night before turning in. Each time, he cursed himself for not being with them when they needed him most.

Like many others, Travis had thought the war would be quick, the South becoming a sovereign nation, and he'd return to his farm. It hadn't worked out the way anyone expected.

Splendor

Baron Ernst Klaussner slid into a black riding jacket, straightening the collar and sleeves, then glanced in the mirror. Satisfied, he picked up his top hat, placing it carefully on his head before grabbing his cane. Leaving his suite of rooms at the St. James Hotel, Ernst took the stairs to the lobby, nodding toward the young man at the front counter.

"May I assist you, Baron?" Thomas's eager expression never changed. He'd started at the hotel when it opened, washing dishes and scrubbing floors before advancing to a server position in the Eagle's Nest restaurant. He'd recently been promoted to working at the front counter.

"Not right now, Thomas."

"Shall I fetch your carriage or horse?"

"I believe I'll walk to the livery myself. I've heard the proprietor, Mr. Brandt, is quite a shootist. Perhaps he'll be agreeable to providing lessons."

Thomas stared at Ernst, debating whether to tell him what most everyone in town already knew. An accomplished sharpshooter for the Union, Noah Brandt had little desire to use a firearm again, unless it meant protecting his family or the town. Deciding to let Noah make his own explanation, Thomas nodded.

"Best of luck, Baron. I hope your discussion goes well."

"Good day to you, Thomas." Stepping out into the noon sun, Ernst drew in a deep breath.

When his father died, Ernst had assumed his role as the new baron, running businesses and properties, leaving little time for the activities he loved. Marrying helped settle him, and when his wife gave birth to their son, Johann, Ernst vowed to teach him all his father had taught him. They'd had little chance to be a family. Within a year of giving birth, his wife died of the fever, driving Ernst into deep despair. Paired with the political turmoil in Austria and Prussia, he'd crossed the Atlantic, bringing his son, servants, and vast fortune with him.

After traveling to New York from Germany, he'd never quite felt comfortable. The city left him unsettled, even if it did offer the social activities he'd learned to appreciate growing up in an aristocratic family.

He'd found a friend in Walter Evans, a well-respected banker and financier. Over time, Ernst revealed his dislike of New York and desire to teach Johann about the outdoors. He had come west at Walter's suggestion, purchasing a ranch near Splendor, including a two-bedroom home, barn, corrals, and excellent pastureland.

Within a week of their arrival, the house had been leveled and plans were drawn for an expansive log structure, one as opulent as any hunting lodge he'd visited in Europe. It wouldn't be long before his new home would be completed, allowing him and Johann to move out of the St. James.

Strolling down the boardwalk, he tipped his hat to an older couple, then a group of young women, and finally, two ranch hands walking into the Dixie. Ernst had become used to the curious stares, no longer considering it rude behavior as he had when he'd first arrived.

"Ernst!"

He shifted to look across the street. Walter Evans came striding toward him, his normally stoic expression replaced with an easy grin.

"Where are you off to in such a hurry?"

Ernst accepted Walter's hand before turning toward the livery. "I've decided to have a word with Mr. Brandt at the livery. I'd like him to instruct me on the use of the American rifle."

Walter's brows scrunched together. "Whatever for? From what you've said, you're an excellent shot."

Ernst nodded. "With German firearms. I want to learn what they use here. I've been told Brandt is the best shot in Splendor."

Walter blew out a slow breath. His son, Gabe, and Noah had grown up together in New York, although Noah's family hadn't been of the same financial status as Gabe's. The two had become as close as brothers. When they were ready to attend college, Walter had funded Noah's education as well as Gabe's. The advent of the war interrupted their education, both leaving to join the Union cause.

Rubbing his neck, Walter glanced at the livery. "Noah is a superb marksman and a patient man. I doubt you'd find a better teacher, except..." He pursed his lips, not sure how to continue.

Ernst lifted a brow. "Except?"

"Being a sharpshooter changed him. Since the war, he picks up a gun to protect his family and friends. Never for sport."

"Ah, yes. I'd forgotten you've known the man since his youth." Ernst clasped Walter on the shoulder. "Then you must come along. Help me convince him to accept my offer."

"I assure you, money won't sway him."

Ernst's gaze narrowed. "He works as a blacksmith and owns a livery. I've never heard of a wealthy man in such a trade."

Shaking his head, Walter chuckled. "All I'll say is Noah married well." Stroking his chin, he glanced between Ernst and the livery, an idea forming. "I have a suggestion. Come on, but allow me to speak with him first."

"Wouldn't it be better to ask Travis to select a horse for you, Isabella?" Noah wiped his hands on an old rag, stuffing it into his back pocket.

"I'd prefer to do this on my own, Noah. Travis and Wyatt are working long hours to fulfill orders for the Army. Now isn't the time to bother him with such a request." Isabella grasped her hands in front of her, hoping Noah didn't hear the tremor in her voice. She had no desire to explain how she and Travis were no longer as close as they'd once been, or that she'd never consider asking him such a favor.

Crossing his arms, Noah studied her face, knowing she hadn't given him a complete answer. Deciding the choice was hers, he looked out the open door to the livery in back.

"I have a mare you might like. How long has it been since you've ridden?"

"Luke lets me use a horse whenever I have the time and desire to ride. Travis usually goes with me, but, well..." She bit her lower lip, swallowing her hesitation. "It's time I have my own horse."

"If you don't want to ask Travis, Luke or Dax would be glad to provide one."

She looked at the ground, then raised her gaze to his. "Please, Noah. I've the money and would very much like to do this on my own."

Letting his arms fall to his sides, he nodded. "Do you have a saddle or bridle?"

"I'd hoped you could help me select those, as well."

Noah had opened a saddlery and leather shop next to the livery, enjoying a brisk business with the local ranchers and many newcomers to Splendor.

"Are you sure about this, Isabella?"

"Yes, I am. I've thought about it quite a bit. It's time for me to start doing more on my own."

Noah's mouth tilted into a grin. "And a horse is the start?"

Seeing the merriment in his eyes, she laughed. "Yes, it is."

"If you're certain, follow me out back and we'll look at the mare." He pushed open the door, allowing her to pass in front of him before walking to a stall at the far end. "Her name is Blossom."

Isabella looked over the top of the stall, her breath catching. "My Lord, Noah. She's beautiful. Where did you get her?"

Resting a hand on the top rail, he shrugged. "From Dax and Luke. Travis trained her for me."

She stepped away from the stall. "You must have had a reason for buying her. I'm sure you have another horse suitable for me."

He looked into the stall. "I hadn't planned to sell her, Isabella." He rubbed his chin. "It will be a couple more years before my son is ready for his own horse and Blossom needs to be ridden. I think she'd be the perfect horse for you. 'Course, that depends on if you want a horse Travis trained." His gaze locked with hers, as if he suspected more than what she'd told him.

Lifting her chin, Isabella nodded. "Blossom is perfect."

"Would you like to ride her before deciding?"

She shook her head. "That's not necessary. If you say Blossom is perfect, I'm certain she is. I'll need everything we discussed, and I don't want you taking less money than you should."

Noah chuckled. He'd already planned to give her a bargain on Blossom. "I'll sell her to you for what she cost me."

Setting her hands on her hips, she gave him a stern look. "You certainly will not. I'll pay you twice what you paid and not a cent less."

Shaking his head, he quoted a price.

"That seems awfully reasonable. You'd better not be fibbing to me, Noah Brandt. I have ways of finding out."

Chuckling, he gave a quick nod toward Blossom. "I'll take fifty dollars more than what I paid and no more, Isabella. Accept it, or I'll keep the horse."

Her lips twitched as she nodded. "It's a deal, Noah." She held out her hand.

He grasped it, giving it a gentle shake. "Now, let's find you a saddle."

Chapter Three

Ernst and Walter waited just inside the blacksmith shop, listening to the conversation between Noah and Isabella. When she held out her hand to Noah, Ernst's brows rose and eyes widened.

"Is that woman completing a business transaction, Walter?"

"Why, yes, I believe she is. I'm learning women are quite independent out west. Much more so than in New York."

"Or Germany. Who is she?"

Walter took Ernst's elbow, drawing him farther into the blacksmith shop. "Mrs. Isabella Boucher. She's a close friend of Gabe's wife, Lena. They've known each other for many years."

"Why wouldn't Mrs. Boucher's husband conduct the transaction? It would seem much more proper."

Walter chuckled. Before the need arose to travel west to speak with Gabe, he would've thought the same. He'd stayed for the wedding of his daughter, Nora, to Wyatt Jackson. Afterward, Walter decided to extend his visit several more weeks, long enough to try to forge a better relationship with his two oldest children. He'd learned a great deal about the men and women who'd chosen to forge a new life in the west.

"Mrs. Boucher's husband died a few years ago. From what I understand, she lives with Luke and Ginny Pelletier at their place a mile or so away from Dax and Rachel. Although she never had children of her own, Lena and Nora tell me she's quite gifted with them."

Ernst's voice lowered. "She's a widow?"

Walter studied his friend's face, seeing more than a casual interest. "Yes, she is. Would you like me to introduce you?"

A solemn expression appeared on Ernst's face. "I would be grateful."

"All right, but I must tell you. I've heard there is a cowhand on the Pelletier ranch who may have an interest in her."

"A cowhand with an interest in a woman of such fine background?" Ernst had the good sense to realize what he'd said an instant before Walter's mouth opened. "I mean no disrespect. I know Nora's husband also works for the Pelletiers."

Walter forced away the anger at someone disparaging his daughter's choice in a husband, realizing the hypocrisy in his reaction. He'd felt the same when Nora first told him who she planned to marry.

"You'll find there are several women of means in Splendor, Ernst. Many have chosen to marry men who make their living with their hands."

Clearing his throat, Ernst nodded. "This way of thinking is quite new to me, Walter. No woman of my class in Germany would've been allowed to marry a man so far beneath her."

Chuckling, Walter gave a crisp nod. "Not so different from where I grew up in New York."

Both men quieted at the sound of voices out front. Turning, they saw Isabella and Noah approach.

"Mr. Evans. I wasn't expecting you today." Noah held out his hand to Walter.

"Noah, I believe you've met Baron Klaussner."

"I have." He shook Ernst's hand, then looked at Isabella. "Have you met Mrs. Boucher, Baron?"

Ernst shook his head. "I've not had the pleasure." He bowed to Isabella. "Mrs. Boucher, I'm Baron Ernst Klaussner."

Her lips curved into a smile. "I'm pleased to meet you, Baron." She shifted her gaze to Noah. "I'll be back in two hours. Will that be enough time?"

Noah nodded. "More than enough."

"Wonderful. I'm quite excited about the purchase." She looked at the other men. "Good day, gentlemen. It was a pleasure to meet you, Baron Klaussner."

Ernst made another bow, then straightened. "Mrs. Boucher."

Watching until she'd continued along the boardwalk, Noah turned to Walter. "What can I do for you?"

Ernst took a step forward. "Actually, I am the one with a request. I understand you are quite the marksman, Mr. Brandt."

Noah's features stilled. He seldom spoke of his expertise as a sharpshooter. Most in Splendor knew better than to ask him about his experience during the war.

"I was a sharpshooter for the Union, Baron, but that was a long time ago."

"Yes, I've heard of your background and that you rarely pick up a weapon any longer."

He studied the man's face, knowing the baron would continue with whatever he had to say. "That's true."

Ernst ignored Noah's warning look. "In any case, I have a proposal for you."

Glancing at Walter, Noah saw him give a slight shrug, an indication for him to at least listen to what Ernst had to say. "What do you want from me?"

"A little of your time. I need instruction on your American weapons, and I believe you're the man to teach me. I've quite a bit of experience from hunting during my youth, but it's been a long time."

Noah's mouth drew into a thin line as he took a moment to consider the request. Shaking his head, he met Ernst's waiting gaze. "Between my businesses and family, I'm afraid I've little time left over."

"I'm willing to pay a generous sum for your time. Plus, I'd like my son, Johann, to learn from you, as well."

Noah had met twelve-year-old Johann. Lena's son, Jack, had befriended the boy soon after his arrival in Splendor, helped him meet other children, and made him feel welcome. He hated to turn the man down.

"Bull Mason is as good a marksman as me."

"Yes, I know of Bull's background. The man is quite busy overseeing the construction of my house and working at the Pelletier ranch." Ernst had made an agreement with Dax, Luke, and Bull about employing him to provide plans for his home. He'd supervise the building and continue his work as one of the foremen at Redemption's Edge.

Letting out a breath, Noah nodded. He knew Bull had little time to provide training to Ernst. "I can spare one day. Meet me here Saturday after breakfast. I'll teach you as much as I can, but we must be finished by noon."

Holding out his hand, a broad smile crossed Ernst's face. "Wonderful, Mr. Brandt. Johann and I will see you Saturday."

Gripping Ernst's hand, Noah glanced at Walter, seeing a satisfied tilt to his mouth. He'd always been close to Gabe's father, respected him, and after all these years, still felt the need to please the man. Providing a few hours to Ernst seemed little in comparison to what Walter had given him.

Even so, as Noah watched them leave, he already regretted his decision.

Redemption's Edge

"I think we have all of them, boys." Travis circled Banjo around the agitated band of wild horses they'd discovered in a nearby canyon. He reined up next to Mal, a ranch hand who'd been with the Pelletiers for a couple years. "You all right leading them back to the ranch?"

Looking over the size of the herd, Mal nodded. "Yep. The boys and me can get them home. Where are you headed?"

Travis looked past him at the mountains to the west. "I'm going to ride over to Solitude Gorge."

Mal knew the spot. "Are you thinking there might be more horses there?"

Shrugging, Travis squinted into the retreating sun. "Maybe. I've seen them there before."

"Then I'll have Tat take this herd back and go with you."

Travis shook his head. "It's a long shot, Mal. If there are horses, it'll be a small herd. I can handle them alone."

Mal studied him, knowing there was more to Travis's desire to go alone than he wanted to say. "If that's what you want. I'll talk with the boys and we'll start back."

Travis helped them form the herd, riding at the back for a hundred yards before reining his horse west. His body relaxed the farther he rode. He found an immense sense of satisfaction in rounding up wild horses and training them to fulfill the Army contracts. Since making the decision about Isabella, he'd found little pleasure in anything. He hoped spending a few hours at what he considered his private spot would refresh him, give him a new sense of himself and a purpose.

Winding up the rocky path, he peered ahead to a narrow valley. Rocky walls rose on both sides, a churning creek splitting the distance between them.

The Frey brothers, two widowers who sold their property to Dax and Luke before moving away, told the story of how a band of Blackfoot had survived a winter between the protective walls of the valley.

Enough game wandered into the narrow passage to provide food during the harsh winter. The ice-covered stream offered an ample supply of water and fish. Many in the small village balked when the time came to move. They'd found solitude and peace between the sheer rock cliffs. Over time, locals began referring to the narrow valley as Solitude Gorge. Travis found himself drawn to it whenever he required time alone, quiet moments to reflect on his life and future.

Stopping at the edge of the stream, he slid from the saddle, ground tying Banjo before kneeling beside the water. Cupping his hands, he drank a liberal amount, then scrubbed his face.

Straightening, he looked around, seeing and hearing nothing. Travis walked back to Banjo, grabbing the gelding's reins. Making his way along a path next to the stream, he allowed himself to think of his wife and daughter. Other than looking at the battered photo each night, he'd worked to push the memories of them aside. The mental images still hurt far too much to dwell on. His guilt at not being with them as they struggled for life would always haunt him, a constant reminder of his failure to protect those he loved.

He'd thought, with time, their laughing faces and cheery voices would fade. Instead, Travis could still close his eyes, seeing them as if they were alive, walking beside him. It was a sick trick of the mind. Whiskey didn't fade the images, nor had his close friendship with Isabella.

Dropping the reins, he leaned against a large rock, allowing himself to relax. It wouldn't be long before the sun descended, obscuring the trail home.

Hearing sounds above him, he lifted his face toward the sky, a slight smile forming at the sight of an eagle soaring a hundred feet above him. Free and unencumbered, the enormous bird represented everything Travis sought. He'd thought freeing Isabella to find someone able to give her the family she desired would provide the peace he sought. It hadn't happened.

Travis had been so sure of his inability to love again, he'd failed to see how much he valued Isabella's friendship, how much he cared. To most, she seemed a genteel easterner with impeccable manners and a quiet nature.

Underneath the façade, he knew she had a core of steel, a strength he'd never been able to find.

No woman since his wife's death had aroused him the same way as Isabella. Although he'd never acted on his desire, he'd wanted her with a passion more fervent than he'd ever felt for his wife. The thought of another woman replacing her sickened him, but his lust for Isabella didn't subside. And, God help him, he'd forced himself to believe lust was all he felt. It had taken driving her away to prove the fallacy in his thinking.

Straightening, he inhaled a deep breath, taking one more look around before swinging atop Banjo. The time in his favorite place hadn't provided firm answers. Instead, it had given him cause to doubt his actions, wondering once again if he'd made the biggest mistake of his life.

Travis had never been a man to make hasty decisions. He chewed on them, worked them over in his mind until he felt satisfied with his choice. Cutting Isabella loose hadn't come as the result of rash thought. He'd pondered it for weeks before she'd confronted him at the ranch. Even so, he hadn't been one hundred percent certain. And the doubts hadn't let up.

With the sun sinking behind him, he took a longer trail back to the ranch, one giving him more time to ponder the dilemma he'd created. Travis felt no urgency to rethink his decision.

Isabella was as careful and steady as him. She'd never rush out to find someone else or feel the need to make changes to her orderly life.

Making a rash decision wouldn't suit anyone. Especially Isabella.

Splendor

"I love her, Noah. She's the perfect horse for me." Isabella felt giddy at the feel of Blossom underneath her. "She responds so well."

Noah's eyes crinkled in amusement as he watched her ride around the corral at his home up the hill from town. "Blossom had a good trainer."

The thought dampened her spirits for a mere instant before she shook the melancholy aside. Travis did a magnificent job with the mare, the same as he did with every horse. She'd have to get used to talking about him, and Isabella refused to let his desire to be alone hinder her future.

"Yes, she did." Turning the mare in the opposite direction, Isabella continued to direct Blossom around the corral until the sun dimmed. Forcing herself to stop, she couldn't help the joy on her face. "If you don't mind, I'd like to ride her to Gabe's for the night. Tomorrow, I'll take her to Luke's."

"Let me saddle Tempest and I'll ride with you." He turned toward the barn.

"You don't need to do that. It isn't very far."

Noah stopped, settling his hands on his waist, giving her an indulgent expression. "No sense arguing, Isabella. There's no chance I'll let you ride there alone on a new horse. Give me a couple minutes and I'll be ready." He opened the gate for her to ride out, then continued to the barn.

She watched him leave, knowing Gabe would be furious with her and his closest friend if he let her ride back in the dark.

"Do you love her?" Noah's wife, Abby, walked up, holding Gabriel's hand as he toddled beside her. At one and a half, he looked like his father, but had his mother's feisty disposition.

Isabella nodded, unable to hide her delight as she guided the horse out of the corral. "Blossom is perfect for me. She has spunk, is the right height, and responds well. I'm so glad I spoke to Noah."

"I wondered who he'd finally give her up to. She deserves to be ridden, not cooped up in the livery until Gabriel is old enough to ride."

Isabella's joy faded a little. "Are you certain you want to part with her?"

Abby nodded. "We've talked about it many times. There will be good horses to choose from when Gabriel is three or four."

Isabella's eyes widened. "Three or four?"

She nodded, chuckling. "That's when I started riding. It's common to start young out here." Her face softened, seeing Noah walking toward them with Tempest.

"I'm going to escort Isabella to Gabe's. I shouldn't be gone long." He bent down, kissing Abby on the cheek.

"Will you be keeping Blossom there?"

Isabella shook her head. "I'll ride her to Luke's tomorrow. He and Ginny still need some help with Cooper, and I do love living at the ranch."

"I know what you mean..." Abby's voice trailed off as she thought of the ranch where she grew up. Her father, King Tolbert, had owned the largest spread in western Montana until his death. With her mother gone, Abby inherited the vast property, as well as many other holdings. She'd made the difficult decision to sell the ranch to the Pelletiers, keeping the other investments.

"You know you're welcome to come out anytime. Ginny takes Coop to visit Rachel several days a week. I'd love the company."

Bending down to pick up Gabriel, Abby looked at her. "I'd love to. Perhaps later this week."

"We'd best get started, Isabella. I don't want Gabe and Lena wondering where you are." Noah swung up onto his horse, holding the reins lightly in his hand.

"Hope to see you soon, Abby." Isabella followed Noah down the short path to town, feeling better than she had in weeks.

She'd made several resolutions since seeing Travis. The first one was to become more independent. Since her husband's death, she'd leaned on the support of Gabe and Lena, the Pelletiers, and Travis, relying on their friendships too much. Buying Blossom liberated her from borrowing horses or buggys to visit friends.

Isabella also decided the time had come to move back to town. Ginny didn't need as much help with Cooper, resulting in many days alone at the ranch with little to do. She knew of a small house not far from the church that would be perfect. It required a little work, but she knew Bull or Noah would help her hire men. After always living with someone else, the thought of her own place excited her more than she imagined.

Isabella no longer wanted to dwell on Travis, spending her time trying to figure out what went wrong. She wasn't young, but she certainly wasn't old. There was no reason she couldn't meet someone else. A man who could love her, wanting to build a life and family. The arrival of the four mail order brides might limit her choices, but she still felt the need to try. She didn't want to go through her life alone, not experiencing love one more time.

Riding through town, she waved at those she knew, thinking of all she wanted to accomplish. She knew the changes wouldn't be enough to clear her heart of Travis. Time and determination would eventually force him from her thoughts.

Instead, she meant to keep busy, enjoy what she had, and make new friends. After all, there must be someone, even in a remote wilderness town, who'd be interested in a relationship and family.

As they passed through town, taking the turn to Gabe's, her heart began to pound, fear trying to dislodge her excitement. Isabella ruthlessly pushed aside her concerns. As she'd told herself when her husband died, she'd take it a day at a time, build a new life, and go on.

The time had come to do just that.

Chapter Four

Philadelphia

David Peeler lowered the brim of his hat, trying to hide himself within the crush of people moving along the street. Carrying a small satchel in his hand, he let out a satisfied breath at his timing. If he wanted to live, he had to be smart...and careful.

Slipping a hand into his coat pocket, he pulled out a ticket, confirming the time. Assuming the next hour went as planned, he'd escape Philadelphia on his way to a new life far away from the men who wanted to destroy him. Men who'd once been close friends and business partners.

Shifting the satchel into his other hand, David jostled the man passing him, earning a sneer and murmured expletive. He ignored the slight. More urgent matters pressed upon him, such as making it to the railroad station without being seen.

David still reeled from the misfortune he and his associates had experienced over the last few years. One poor decision had turned into two, then three. They'd all voted on each, but over time, the blame had fallen on him.

He'd been the one to pull them all together into what had become a lucrative partnership, four golden boys turning their already substantial wealth into enviable fortunes. Mansions, racehorses, trips to Europe, and a succession of beautiful women made them the envy of many. It had also brought unwanted attention from connivers and those who sought to knock them down.

David still didn't understand why they'd all turned on him. He may have made a few mistakes, but no more than the others. Every one of them lost money, none more than him. The fact they still wouldn't be destitute didn't assuage their anger. They'd made David the scapegoat, the object of irrational hostility. It was a role he hadn't earned and refused to accept.

The four were scheduled to meet tonight over drinks. David snorted at the thought. He knew what they intended. It would be a tribunal, a conviction of what they saw as his failings. David had no intention of playing their game. By the time they realized he wouldn't be attending, he'd be miles along the tracks, sipping a whiskey, knowing they'd never be able to humiliate him again.

"If you'll sign here, Mrs. Brandt, we'll be finished and you may continue on with your day." Albert Payson slid the paper across the desk, then handed her a pen.

Taking it, Abby held Gabriel on her lap, holding back a grin at Albert's stiff posture and formal manner. His brother, Ernest, moved from Big Pine a few years before to help her sort out the substantial investments her father had made before his death. She liked Ernie, finding him amusing and less stiff than his younger brother.

Scribbling her signature, she handed back the pen and paper. "How is your brother doing, Mr. Payson?"

"Ernie is doing well. Glad to be back in Boston. Although, by the tone of his letters, I do believe he misses it here."

"And how do you like Splendor?" She'd heard rumors he'd moved out west to join Ernie in his law practice, only to discover his brother was looking for a replacement, not a partner.

He pursed his lips, as if deciding how much to say to one of his biggest clients. "It's an adjustment. I will say there is much more work here than I first thought. You, Mr. and Mrs. Evans, and the Barnetts keep me busy with your ideas for growth. My guess is Splendor will be the darling of the west in no time."

Abby chuckled at the thought. Her father would've found it quite plausible, if not inevitable.

"One day, this town may be the capital of the state." He closed his mouth with a firm nod.

"Perhaps, Mr. Payson. First, we have to vote to become a state. Before that, we'd have to replace Big Pine as the territorial capital."

"I hope I'm here to see it, Mrs. Brandt." Reading over the document once more, Albert looked up. "What plans do you have for the day?"

She set Gabriel down, allowing him to wander several feet away. "We're riding out to Luke and Ginny Pelletier's house to see Mrs. Boucher. She bought a horse from Noah this week and I'm anxious to see how she's doing."

His brow lifted as he cleared his throat. "Mrs. Boucher. Yes, I've done some work for her. I, uh, heard..."

Abby cocked her head to the side when his voice trailed off. "You heard what, Mr. Payson?"

An uncomfortable look passed across his face before he cleared his throat a second time. "Well, I heard a ranch hand at the Pelletier ranch was courting her."

Abby considered her words. She didn't want to say anything that might cause Isabella any pain. "She has a friend who works for Dax and Luke, but as far as I know, their friendship isn't what you might describe as courting. You may want to consider asking Isabella outright. I promise you, she wouldn't feel offended."

He shook his head. "Oh, no. I couldn't possibly impose on her privacy."

Abby bit her bottom lip to keep from smiling. "Might you have an interest in her, Mr. Payson?"

Albert drew in a deep breath, not quite making eye contact with her. "She is a wonderful lady and quite beautiful. Do you think she might consider having supper with me some evening?"

"I think she might enjoy an evening with you. Would you like me to inquire when I see her today?"

He shifted in his chair, his pale face flushing. "I wouldn't want to put you in an awkward position, Mrs. Brandt."

"Believe me, it wouldn't be awkward at all. In fact, I'd quite enjoy seeing Isabella get out more, have some fun." She studied Albert. "You *are* planning to show her a fun evening, right?"

His features stiffened, as if she'd slapped him. "Of course. I'll take her to the Eagle's Nest for supper, then perhaps to Ruby's Palace for the floor show."

Abby's eyes widened. Everyone knew Ruby's girls put on a wonderful show each evening.

Perhaps Albert didn't know the other services her girls offered after the performance ended.

"Well, it would certainly be something different, Mr. Payson. If you're agreeable, I'll mention it to her today." Standing, she walked to Gabriel, who busied himself with a heavy doorstop. Picking him up, she turned back to Albert. "Please let me know if my offer is accepted."

Albert stood, giving a slight nod. "As soon as I hear back. And, uh…thank you for speaking with Mrs. Boucher on my behalf."

"It will be my pleasure."

Redemption's Edge

Slapping his hat against his thigh, Mal tossed it onto his bunk. "I'm mighty glad it's Saturday, boys. Anyone interested in supper at Suzanne's before going to Ruby's for the show?"

Five men responded right away, including Tat and Johnny. Travis unbuttoned his shirt, tossing it onto the bunk before scrubbing a hand down a face etched with fatigue.

"How about you, Travis?" Tat slapped him on the back. "It's about time you got away from here for a while."

Travis didn't go with the men often, preferring to spend time alone or visiting Isabella. He didn't want to do the first and couldn't do the second. The thought had him wondering what she'd be doing tonight and with whom she'd be spending her time. Luke and Ginny were having supper with Dax and Rachel, and Bull had told him Gabe, Lena, and Walter Evans were eating at the Eagle's Nest. If true, it meant Isabella would be alone. The thought twisted his heart.

Tat snapped his fingers in front of Travis's face. "Are you coming with us?"

He let out a frustrated breath. "Sure. Give me a few minutes to clean up."

Travis couldn't allow himself to dwell on Isabella any longer. Getting off the ranch with the boys would be good for him, clear his head. He had no plans to do more than spend time away and have supper at Suzanne's. As entertaining as he found them, watching Ruby's girls perform didn't appeal to him.

Tat let out a whoop. "Then get moving. We've got a big night ahead of us."

The instant Abby stopped by to let him know Isabella was agreeable to supper, Albert Payson had closed the office and rode to Luke's ranch. Feeling as young as a schoolboy, he refused to allow any time to pass before inviting her to dine with him on Saturday.

Isabella had surprised him by ordering a large steak, foregoing the vegetables for a double portion of mashed potatoes. Albert enjoyed every minute, watching her devour her food as they compared stories of growing up back east. He found her unpretentious, modest, and utterly delightful. The women he'd known in Boston couldn't compare to Isabella's unaffected manner.

"Do you plan to stay in Splendor, Mr. Payson?" She scooped up a spoonful of cobbler, closing her eyes as she savored the taste. Sensing his gaze on her, she opened her eyes, taking a quick lick of the spoon before setting it down.

The action, so unexpected and unladylike, caused Albert to slip a finger inside the collar of his shirt, stifling a groan.

"Are you all right?" Isabella leaned forward, her brows furrowing.

Feeling his face heat, Albert nodded. "Yes, of course. However, it does seem a little warm in here."

Straightening, she cocked her head. "I'm quite comfortable. Perhaps if you removed your coat."

He shook his head, clearing his throat. "No, I'm fine." Shifting in his chair, Albert took a sip of coffee. "You seem to be enjoying your dessert."

Her eyes gleamed. "It's wonderful. Gabe did a marvelous job selecting the chef for the restaurant. There are times I think his talent is wasted as the sheriff."

"When I met with his father, Mr. Evans made it clear he thought Gabe should move back to New York, take over the hotels his uncle left and forget about living in such a violent world."

Isabella choked on the cobbler, picking up her coffee to take a swallow. "Walter said that?" She didn't wait for Albert to respond. "Well, of course he did. It's always been easy for him to ignore the violence in his hometown. When you live so far removed from the sordid part of life, I suppose you're able to pretend it doesn't exist."

He nodded. "Boston also has a good amount of crime. I've found Splendor to be much more peaceful, the people more accepting than those back home." Seeing she'd finished her cobbler and coffee, he leaned toward her. "Would you care to see the performance at Ruby's this evening?"

Her eyes widened. "Ruby's Grand Palace?" Isabella's voice held a hint of excitement.

"Well, yes. I understand the actresses perform a variety show on Saturday nights. Singing, dancing, humorous skits."

"You haven't been there?"

He shook his head, beginning to doubt his choice of entertainment. "I've been too busy. I thought tonight might be the perfect time, unless you'd prefer for me to take you home."

Isabella's excitement rose. When Lena asked Gabe to take her, he'd refused, saying it wasn't a place for a lady. She'd laughed at him, reminding her husband she'd grown up in a brothel, as did her good friend, Nick Barnett. Gabe had held firm, much to Lena's amusement. Isabella suspected her friend had already stopped by to see Ruby's entertainment for herself.

"I'd love to go."

Standing, he stepped behind her, pulling out her chair. "I do believe this is going to be a memorable evening, Mrs. Boucher."

"One more round before we go to Ruby's." Tat held up his hand, getting the barmaid's attention.

After finishing supper at Suzanne's, they'd moved to the Dixie for whiskey before the show.

"Not for me." Travis stood, reaching into his pocket, tossing coins onto the table.

"And miss the show?" Johnny's voice rose above the noise in the saloon.

Chuckling, Travis nodded. "Maybe another time." Slapping his hat onto his head, he walked to the door, coming to an abrupt halt. He couldn't quite believe what he saw on the other side of the street.

A couple walked at a slow pace, turning to move between two buildings. Travis knew all they'd find on the next street would be a few houses, the clinic, and Ruby's Grand Palace.

What stalled his breath, slamming into him with the force of a physical blow, was the identity of the woman. Isabella.

Knowing he shouldn't, Travis stepped onto the street, intent on following the pair. If he wasn't mistaken, he knew the man accompanying her. Albert Payson, the attorney who handled her business and that of most others in town. He'd never had need of the man's services, but understood people regarded him as quite capable and smart. And unmarried. The last caused Travis's pace to surge.

Moving between the buildings, he stopped where the passage met the next street. He felt his anger rise as Payson escorted Isabella to the door of Ruby's Grand Palace, opening it for her to enter in front of him.

Muttering a curse, he waited until they'd gone inside, then moved to the entrance. Before he could open the door, the sound of laughter came from behind him. Mal, Tat, Johnny, and the others strolled across the street.

"Look who changed his mind." Johnny clasped him on the shoulder, chuckling.

Shoving hands into his pockets, he nodded. "I thought it would be good to come by for one drink, see at least part of the show."

Mal stepped next to him. "Well, I'm glad you decided to stay. Might be I'll head back with you."

Since Wyatt, the ranch hand he felt closest to, married Nora and moved to town, Travis spent a good deal of his evenings playing cards and talking with Mal. He liked the man, valued his counsel about cattle and ranching.

"Sounds good."

"Well, let's stop gabbing and get inside before we miss the show." Tat pulled the door open, holding it until all the men entered the darkened interior.

Travis blinked several times, letting his eyes adjust to the dimly lit room. A good number of customers turned to look at the group, some waving when they recognized the men from

Redemption's Edge. He trailed behind, trying to locate Isabella without her noticing him.

The place seemed bigger inside. Paintings of scantily clad women adorned the walls. Numerous chandeliers hung from the high ceiling, providing meager light for the tables below. A band made up of four members sat to the right of the stage, playing tunes he didn't recognize. A red velvet curtain spanned the wide stage, light peeking out from underneath.

The sound of furniture scraping across the floor drew his attention. The men moved two tables together, shifting chairs so they all had a good view of the stage. Travis took the chair farthest away from the other customers, his back to the wall as he continued to survey the room. It took mere seconds for him to find her and Payson at a table a row from the front, leaning toward each other, talking.

He couldn't stop the irritation rising within him. Gripping the arms of the chair, he tried to relax, control the anger at seeing her with another man.

Travis knew his feelings were irrational. After all, he'd been the one to set Isabella free, telling her they had no future. He hadn't expected to find her inside Ruby's a week later, another man by her side, waiting for a show he knew she shouldn't see.

His thoughts were disrupted when the music changed to a tune he recognized, loud and raucous, one he'd expect from a place such as Ruby's. The curtain parted enough for Ruby to step through, raising her hands in greeting, a broad smile on her face. The music stopped when she began to speak.

"Ladies and gents, welcome to Ruby's Grand Palace. You are in for a treat tonight." She halted as the crowd, made up mostly of men, hooted and hollered, a few whistling. "My girls have been practicing long hours to make sure you have an evening you'll not soon forget." Again, the shouts started, dying down when she raised her hand. "Now, who's ready for great music and beautiful women?" This time, she allowed the cheers to go on for a few minutes, then signaled for the band to start again.

When they reached a crescendo, the curtains opened, revealing a line of women clad in short, bawdy dresses, hair piled high on their heads, stockings covering their legs, black dancing shoes on their feet.

"May I present the ladies of Ruby's Grand Palace." Ruby waved her arm toward the ladies as she made her way off stage.

Travis's gaze moved to Isabella. She'd leaned forward, her lips slightly parted, eyes wide as the women began to kick and prance to the music. He doubted she'd ever seen anything like it and wished she wasn't being exposed to it tonight.

A wave of protectiveness gripped him, his hands tightening even more on the arms of his chair. When Payson's hand moved to the small of her back, Travis lost control. He pushed back the chair, meaning to stand, when Mal's hand on his arm stilled his movements.

"You need to get yourself together, Travis. It wouldn't be right to kill a man inside Ruby's."

He looked at his friend, his nostrils flaring. Had he been that transparent?

"I've got a pretty good idea what you're feeling, but believe me, now isn't the time to make a commotion about who Miss Isabella is with." Mal's grip tightened. "Relax, have a drink, and enjoy the show. We both know that woman isn't going to do something foolish. There'll be another time to sort this all out."

Letting out a breath, Travis nodded. Mal was right. He had to get control of himself. The only outcome of a confrontation would be for one of the deputies, or Gabe himself, to haul him to jail, humiliating Isabella and making him look the fool. Which he'd be if he started anything tonight.

"I'm good," he murmured, glad no one else at their table heard Mal's words.

"Let's have that drink and get out of here. You'll figure this out when you've had time to clear your head."

Travis hoped so because, right now, he felt like tearing Ruby's down, to hell with the consequences.

Chapter Five

St. Louis, Missouri

David looked around the crowded room, an involuntary shiver running through him as he studied his surroundings. The rustic building where he took his meal couldn't compare to the opulent restaurants in Philadelphia, nor could the food.

Pulling out his pocket watch, David checked the time. Another hour before the train left for Omaha. He'd been watching other passengers as they entered and exited the train, searching for anyone who might be connected to his associates back east. No one looked familiar or appeared to be searching for him.

"More coffee?" The harried server hovered over him.

Nodding, David drummed his fingers on the table as the young man filled his cup. "Is it always this busy?"

"It is when the train arrives." He glanced behind him, seeing several more people enter the restaurant, then looked back at David. "Anything else?"

He didn't hear the question, his attention focused on a man taking a seat several tables away. "Do you know the man with the black bowler?" David nodded in the direction of the man.

The server took a quick look behind him. "The one sitting alone?"

"Yes."

"No, sir. I've never seen him before. So, can I get you anything else?"

David shook his head. "No. This will be fine."

Grabbing the newspaper from the chair beside him, David held it up, using it as a shield to study the man. The stranger showed no interest in anything except ordering a meal. He never looked in David's direction or took notice of anyone around him.

Shaking his head, he lowered the paper, feeling a little foolish. His associates couldn't have discovered his disappearance and mounted a search in such a short time. By the time they realized he'd emptied his bank account and left Philadelphia, David was already hundreds of miles away. They'd have no idea what direction he traveled or his ultimate destination.

Although his business associates had become friends, he'd never fully trusted them. None knew of his connection to anyone outside their circle. He'd been careful to keep the name of his personal attorney separate from their joint business dealings, the same as he'd kept money in a bank different from the one their partnership used.

David's banker believed him to be paranoid. The man's opinion never mattered as long as he took care of his money. Keeping his affairs private meant more to David than what others thought. Sipping his coffee, he felt a grin tug at the corners of his mouth. In his case, suspicion might save his life.

Splendor

Lena finished the last square of the quilt she'd been working on for months, a satisfied smile on her face as she set it aside. Picking up her tea, she looked out the side window of the parlor, glad Gabe suggested she take a day off.

As a partner in several businesses with her husband and their friends, the Barnetts, Lena tended to overdo, forgoing sleep to ensure all their affairs ran smoothly. Before Nora's marriage to Wyatt, she'd lived with them, helping with Jack, the meals, and so much more. Lena hadn't realized how much Gabe's sister contributed to running the house until she'd moved out. He'd suggested they hire someone to help, do the chores Nora had done. Lena balked at the idea of having someone she didn't know living in their house, trusting her with their son. She also knew something had to be done.

One of the mail order brides might be perfect. Tapping a finger against her lips, she thought about which one would fit. Her mind flitted through each one. May Bacon worked in the kitchen at the St. James Hotel, Sylvia Lucero helped at the general store, and Tabitha assisted Suzanne at the boardinghouse. That left Deborah Chestro. Lena groaned at the thought of the strong-willed, outspoken young woman having an influence on Jack. Of the four, Deborah would be Lena's last choice.

A sharp tap on the front door startled her from her thoughts. Standing, she walked to the entry, pulling open the door.

"Baron Klaussner. What a nice surprise. Please, come inside. Are you looking for Gabe?"

Removing his hat, he made a slight bow, looking into the house as he moved past her.

"Good morning, Mrs. Evans. I was wondering if Mrs. Boucher might be here this morning."

She tilted her head, a brow lifting. "Why, no, she isn't. Isabella lives with Luke and Ginny Pelletier." Lena gestured toward the parlor. "Please, have a seat. May I get you some coffee or tea?"

Ernst shook his head. "No, thank you, Mrs. Evans. I believe I'll ride out to the Pelletier's. Do you think Mrs. Boucher, well...would she be agreeable to a visit from me?"

Lena kept her features even, ignoring how the normally confident and assertive baron hesitated on his question. "Isabella is one of the most gracious people I know. I'm certain she'd welcome a visit, Baron."

An almost imperceptible grin appeared. "Wonderful. Then I'll ride out directly." Making another slight bow, he held out his hand to take hers, lifting it to his lips. "Thank you, Mrs. Evans. I appreciate your help." He didn't wait for Lena to walk him to the door before leaving, taking a brisk pace down the steps to his buggy. Climbing onto the seat, he gave Lena a quick nod before slapping the lines.

"Well, well..." she mumbled, acknowledging the somewhat giddy excitement the baron showed at being encouraged to visit Isabella. First Albert Payson, now Baron Klaussner. She didn't believe her friend had ever received so much attention, and Lena couldn't think of any woman who deserved it more.

She knew Isabella had much deeper feelings for Travis than she wanted to admit. Lena saw the love on her face whenever she was with him, witnessed the despair when he gave her his decision about being no more than friends. Isabella would never admit it, but Travis turning away devastated her, destroying what she believed to be a future with the taciturn ranch hand.

Her friend no longer had reason to despair. Two suitors. Who knew how many others might have an interest in Isabella.

As she walked inside, closing the door, Lena wondered what Travis would think if he knew how many men held an interest in the woman he let slip from his grasp.

Redemption's Edge

"How long has Travis been at it?" Luke Pelletier stood next to Wyatt, his arms resting on the top rail of the fence.

Wyatt kept watch on his friend, who'd been in the corral since before dawn. "Too long."

"He needs to take a break and get something to eat."

Wyatt didn't shift his gaze from Travis. "I've tried talking to him twice. He says he's not hungry."

Luke's mouth twisted, indicating his displeasure. "How many has he worked today?"

"Five mares. I've never seen anyone as focused on getting results in such a short time." Wyatt removed his hat, swiping an arm across his forehead.

Resting his chin on his arms, Luke followed Travis's actions, looking for signs of fatigue. "Is he taking shortcuts?"

Wyatt knew what the boss asked. Luke wanted to know if whatever drove Travis caused him to be abusive or cruel.

"He's under control, if that's what you're asking."

Both men lapsed into silence, waiting while Travis finished with the current mare, riding her around the corral before sliding off. Opening the gate, Luke strolled toward him, reaching out to take the reins.

"I'll take her from here. You're due for a break and food."

Travis settled hands on his lean hips, his jaw tight. "I'm fine, Luke."

He narrowed his eyes. "No, you're not. I don't know what's eating at you, but I do know when a man's had enough."

Shaking his head, Travis blew out a frustrated breath. "Look, boss. I—"

"I'm not asking you, Travis. I'm telling you to get yourself out of the corral. Eat, take a ride...hell, I don't care what you do as long as you don't work another horse for at least an hour."

Travis opened his mouth to respond, stopping when he saw the hard look in Luke's eyes. Mumbling a curse, he stormed from the corral, pushing past Wyatt. His uncharacteristic anger caught the attention of several ranch hands, causing them to stop what they were doing and watch him stalk to the pasture where Banjo lifted his head.

One sharp whistle and Travis's horse trotted toward him. Grabbing a bridle hanging over the fence, he settled it over the horse's face, then swung up on the gelding's back, rolling his heels into Banjo's side. A moment later, they were in full motion, Travis's strong thighs holding him firm as they rounded a corner and disappeared.

"Find out what's bothering him."

Wyatt cast a look at Luke. "I'll try, but you know Travis."

Shaking his head, Luke scrubbed a hand down his face. "It's Isabella."

Crossing his arms, Wyatt nodded. "That's my guess. He saw her with another man Saturday night. Mal had to hold him back from beating the tar out of him."

Luke's brows scrunched together. "Who was she with?"

Wyatt snorted. "Albert Payson. One punch and the man would've been laid up for a month."

Chuckling, Luke shook his head. "Seems to me Travis needs to make a decision. Either get her back or purge her from his system. And he needs to do it soon."

Travis rode at a furious pace, reining Banjo north into open pastures stretching for miles. With no destination in mind, he continued toward a large cattle herd, ignoring the men who raised their hands in greeting.

Slowing to a trot, he took a trail west toward Wildfire Creek. The summer heat didn't slow the water's flow, which continued to swell from melting snow in the higher elevations. Moving around the dense brush, he reined to a stop at the edge of the water, swinging his right leg over Banjo's neck and sliding to the ground.

Tossing his hat aside, Travis knelt, scooping up handfuls of water and splashing it over his face. He scrubbed until his skin felt raw. Leaning back, he shook his head and took a deep breath, hoping the churning anger dogging him since seeing Isabella at Ruby's would diminish.

Travis had no explanation for the rush of emotions claiming him when he saw her with

Albert. Isabella was his, or she had been until he pushed her away. The decision had been his, and he deserved every bit of regret flowing through him.

Until he saw her with another man, Travis hadn't been certain of his feelings. He had to accept the truth. Isabella meant more to him than he'd been able to admit, more than he wanted her to. Unable to acknowledge he loved her, Travis settled for realizing he cared a great deal, enough to feel the loss to the depths of his being.

And he knew she felt the same for him. He'd been blinded by the past, afraid of his ability to love after losing his wife and daughter.

The emptiness claiming him now was as consuming as the despair he felt after arriving home to learn he'd lost his family. His hands fisted at his sides. Raising his face to the sky, he opened his mouth. An uncharacteristic scream broke from his lips, the force burning his lungs, tightening his throat.

Allowing himself to feel the pain he'd worked hard to ignore, Travis continued his agonized shout, moisture building in his eyes and streaming down his face. After a while, his voice cracked and he lowered his head. Sucking in deep gulps of air, he felt his body tremble as his hands continued to clench and unclench at his sides.

Sitting on the ground, he rested his arms on bent knees. Travis didn't know how long he stayed there, staring across the creek into the distance. An hour, maybe two. The length of time didn't matter.

What did matter was the realization he may have lost the one person who could help him put the past behind him and build a future. He still didn't know about love. Worse, he had no idea how to get her back or if she'd ever consider giving him another chance.

Seeing her with Payson had been a slap in the face, a blow he hadn't seen coming.

Pushing up, he stood, shredding hands through his hair. He bent down to pick up his hat, carefully placing it on his head as he thought of what to do next.

Isabella hadn't visited Rachel since their last meeting. He had no doubt her absence was intentional. Travis didn't blame her.

She might not want to take a chance on him again, but he'd never know if he didn't try. If she wouldn't come to the ranch, he'd go to her. And Travis knew he had to do it soon.

Chapter Six

Noah watched Johann lift the rifle and aim, the weight of the weapon forcing the boy's arms to tremble. The .45 caliber Spencer repeating rifle could be a friend to those familiar with its use, a foe to anyone unaccustomed to the formidable weapon.

"Aim as I taught you, Johann. When you're certain you have the target, squeeze the trigger."

Nodding, the boy anchored the rifle against his shoulder, his eyes narrowing to slits. Firing, he rocked backward, the recoil too much for his slim frame. Steadying himself, Johann peered into the distance, letting out a frustrated breath. The target remained in place.

It had been the same last week. Miss after miss, always shooting far above the target. So far, Johann had yet to hit his mark.

"You were close that time. This time, I want you to aim below where you see the target."

Johann frowned. "Below?"

"You have to make adjustments for the recoil of the rifle. Each time you fire, the gun rises, causing you to miss. I want you to try lowering your aim."

Glancing at his father standing a few yards away, Johann shrugged, then lifted the rifle.

Positioning himself behind him, Noah watched where the boy aimed. "A little lower, Johann. That's it. Now, let out a breath and squeeze the trigger."

He did as Noah instructed, then fired. Hearing a cracking sound, Johann looked up, shocked to see he'd hit the target.

He looked behind him, a broad smile on his face. "I did it, Father."

Ernst stepped forward, a proud gleam in his eyes. "You certainly did." He clasped his son's shoulder. "Can you do the same to the other targets?"

"I'll try."

Noah moved behind him. "Do exactly as you did the last time. A few inches lower, let out a breath, and fire."

Johann shot four more times, hitting each of the remaining targets.

"Excellent. I don't believe you or your father need any further instruction. What you need to do now is practice."

Johann's brows furrowed. "Are you certain, Mr. Brandt? What if I forget what you taught me?"

Noah grinned. "I think you'll do fine. You're a smart boy and a quick learner. If you do forget, all you have to do is stop by the livery and I'll explain everything again."

Ernst stepped next to them, extending his hand. "Thank you, Mr. Brandt. You've done all I'd hoped."

Noah grasped the baron's hand. "You were a much more accomplished shooter than you let on, Baron. And Johann's smart and has the desire to learn. With practice, I expect he'll be an expert in no time."

"I'm organizing a hunt. Johann, Walter Evans, and his grandson, Jack. I'd very much like you to join us."

Pursing his lips, Noah shook his head. "I appreciate the invitation, Baron. Right now, I've too much work."

"Perhaps sometime in the future then."

Noah hadn't been hunting in over a year. He knew Abby would appreciate something other than beef, chicken, and pork to eat. If the hunt was successful, he'd be able to offer the extra meat to Gabe for use at the Eagle's Nest.

"Perhaps."

After packing the extra ammunition away, they mounted their horses for the short ride back to town.

"Tell me, Mr. Brandt. Where would you suggest we hunt?"

Glancing at Ernst, Noah rubbed his chin. "The best hunting is north of Redemption's Edge. Deer and elk are plentiful, but you have to keep watch for the Blackfoot village. It's about half a day's ride beyond the ranch's border. They're known to hunt farther north of their camp, but they'll go wherever the game is plentiful."

"Will they attack us, Mr. Brandt?" Johann's voice held a mixture of fear and excitement.

"The chief is Running Bear. He's a friend of mine, as well as Bull Mason and the Pelletiers. I consider him to be a good man. But if he feels his people are in danger, he'll protect them by whatever means possible. I'd recommend you hunt within a mile or two of the Pelletier's northern border. Stay well south of where you might encounter the Blackfoot. There's no sense in provoking them."

Ernst looked at Noah. "You say this chief is a friend of Bull's?"

Noah nodded, remembering the bond Bull and Running Bear had formed a while back when Lydia had been kidnapped by a group of renegades. "Yes, he is."

"Then perhaps I'll invite him to join us as a guide."

"You're welcome to ask. From what I've seen, between his duties at the ranch and his work for you, he may not be free to get away."

Noah had heard about the baron's hunting trips. They were rumored to be a spectacle rivaling any small town parade. He insisted on taking his private carriage, as well as a supply wagon loaded with enough food and ammunition to last at least four days. His private chef and another servant always came along, making certain the trip lived up to the baron's high standards. Noah would bet his best gelding Bull wouldn't commit to several days away from his duties.

"Quite true, Mr. Brandt. Nevertheless, I feel compelled to invite him."

Noah kept the smile off his face. What he'd give to see Bull on one of the baron's hunts. It would certainly be worth the loss of a gelding.

Omaha, Nebraska

"Mr. Peeler, we've arrived at our stop." The conductor touched David's shoulder. "Mr. Peeler?"

Blinking, David opened his eyes, looking up at the man. "Thank you."

Straightening in his seat, he glanced outside, seeing *Omaha* on the station sign. Using the armrests, he pushed himself up, grabbing his hat and satchel before following the other passengers outside.

He didn't waste time asking for directions to the nearest restaurant as he had at the other stops. David needed to stretch his legs, take a look at the town he'd heard about from one of his seat mates on the train.

Much larger than anticipated, David strolled the main street, looking at the various shops. He wondered if his destination had as many establishments, if it thrived as Omaha did.

"Excuse me."

David turned to look at the man beside him. "Yes?"

"I believe we've met."

His heart began to pound, his palms growing damp. "I'm sorry, but I don't recognize you."

"By chance are you from Philadelphia?"

David's throat constricted. "Uh, no. New York."

The man shook his head. "I was certain we'd met before." He held out his hand. "Well, sorry to have bothered you, Mr..."

Grasping his hand, David cleared his throat. "Jones. William Jones."

"Well, it was good to meet you, Mr. Jones." The man studied him another moment before turning away.

Feet rooted in place, it took David several moments to realize the man never offered his own name. A shiver of concern rippled through him.

Although he didn't recognize him, his instincts warned him the man knew his true identity, had followed him from Philadelphia.

"But that couldn't be," David mumbled to himself. He'd boarded the train long before his associates could've realized he'd left. At each stop, he'd disembarked long enough to eat, then returned to the train, never interrupting the trip for an overnight stay. He sucked in a shaky breath, telling himself it wasn't possible anyone could've found him so quickly.

Looking down the boardwalk, David spotted a saloon. He needed a drink, maybe more than one, before returning to the train.

Splendor

Ernst removed his hat before knocking on Gabe's front door. He felt awkward, a little unsettled. It had been years since he'd asked a woman to supper. When he'd visited Isabella earlier in the week, he'd been enchanted enough to invite her to join him. To his surprise, she agreed.

Gabe opened the door. "Good evening, Baron. Please, come on inside."

"Sheriff. I trust you and Mrs. Evans are well." Ernst hesitated a moment. "And your father, of course."

Closing the door, Gabe nodded. "We're all fine. I understand you've invited Isabella to join you for supper."

"I did. Is she here?"

"Isabella and Lena are upstairs. I doubt it will be long. Why don't you join me for a drink while you wait." Gabe motioned for Ernst to follow him into the study. "Whiskey?"

Fingering the brim of his hat, he nodded before taking a seat. "Thank you."

"Ah, there you are, Ernst." Walter joined them, taking the drink Gabe offered. "Lena told me you're taking Isabella to supper." Sitting next to him, he tilted his glass toward his friend. "An excellent idea. She's a fine woman."

Shifting in his seat, Ernst took a sip of whiskey, wiping a damp hand down his pants. "Yes, she is." He turned his head, looking toward the stairs.

Walter glanced at Gabe, then back at Ernst, his eyes dancing with amusement. "I assume you'll be taking her to the Eagle's Nest."

Forcing his attention back to Walter, Ernst nodded. "Yes, of course."

Gabe stood at a knock on the front door. "Excuse me." Leaving Ernst and his father, he stepped out of the study, glancing at the stairs, seeing no sign of the women. Opening the door, his jaw dropped.

"Good evening, Gabe. I hope I'm not interrupting anything." Travis stood on the porch, wearing his best shirt and pants. "I, uh...rode over to Luke's to see Isabella. He told me she left to stay with you and Lena tonight. Is she here?"

Stepping onto the porch, Gabe shut the door. "Is she expecting you?"

Travis shook his head, his throat working. "No, she isn't."

Scrubbing a hand down his face, Gabe looked away for a moment, then back at Travis. "She's upstairs with Lena." When Travis took a step forward, he held up a hand. "Baron Klaussner is inside. She accepted an invitation to have supper with him."

Travis absorbed the news, his jaw tightening. "I see." His fingers tightened on the brim of his hat. "I'd best be going." Giving Gabe a curt nod, he turned to leave.

"Travis?"

He stopped, glancing over his shoulder.

"It's just supper. Why don't you ride in for church tomorrow? She's staying with us for Sunday meal. You could join us."

Letting out a slow breath, Travis nodded once more before returning to the buggy he'd borrowed from Dax. Watching him drive away, Gabe winced, shaking his head before going back inside to find the women, Ernst, and his father standing in the foyer.

Lena stepped next to him, slipping her arm through his. "Who was that?"

Gabe looked at Isabella. "Travis. He asked for you."

Moving past him, Isabella opened the door, finding the porch empty. "Where is he?"

Leaning down, Gabe lowered his voice. "He left when I told him the baron was taking you to supper." He didn't miss the way her shoulders slumped at the news. "I asked him to join us for church and supper tomorrow."

She glanced up at him, hope shining in her eyes. "Did he agree?"

"Not in so many words. It doesn't mean he won't be there."

Isabella looked away, her gaze focused on the trail back to town. "He won't come."

"How do you know?"

Biting her lower lip, she let out a ragged breath. "I don't know. It's just a feeling." Turning around, she walked back into the house, the excitement she'd felt earlier fading. Shoving aside her disappointment, Isabella straightened her spine, squaring her shoulders as she approached Ernst.

He tilted his head toward her. "Is everything all right, Mrs. Boucher?"

She shot a look at Lena, then nodded. "Yes, Baron. Everything is fine."

"Good. Then we'll be off." Nodding at the others, he held out his arm, waiting until Isabella slipped hers through it.

Gabe closed the door behind them, his mind still on Travis.

Lena touched his arm. "You did the right thing, telling him about the baron."

"He took it pretty well, considering he'd ridden to Luke's, then here." To his surprise, Lena smiled. "What are you thinking?"

"I'm hoping Travis finally figured out his feelings for Isabella. If so, that would be wonderful news." She walked toward the kitchen, glancing into the study to see Walter pouring himself another whiskey.

"Hold on. What if she's changed her mind?"

Walking back to him, she stood on her toes, placing a kiss on Gabe's cheek. "If I know Isabella, that's not even a remote possibility."

Isabella stared down at her plate, listening as Ernst spoke of his home in Germany. He had many stories, all interesting, yet none could hold her attention. All she could think about was Travis, wondering why he'd ridden all the way to town to see her.

Several weeks had gone by without a word. For him to show up as he did, he must've had something important to say.

"And what about you, Mrs. Boucher? Did you grow up in Philadelphia?"

Her gaze shot up to meet his. "Um, no. I moved there to marry my husband."

"Is that where you met Mrs. Evans?"

She shook her head. "No. We were friends for a long time before I met my husband. It was hard leaving her, but she and Nick Barnett had built a good business with plans for more."

"Nick Barnett? He's married to Suzanne, who owns the boardinghouse, correct?"

She smiled. "He is. Nick came here to open the Dixie, and took a room at her place. It took a bit of time for him to express his interest."

"I would've thought Mr. Barnett would've married Lena Evans." Ernst picked up his coffee, taking a sip.

Her brows lifted. "Never. They're very close, but have always seen each other as brother and sister. It all worked out for the best. Gabe is perfect for Lena, and the same holds true for Nick and Suzanne."

Ernst set down his cup, leaning forward. "And you, Mrs. Boucher. Is there someone perfect for you?"

Isabella shifted in her bed, the same as she had for the last few hours. Thoughts of Travis and the reason for his visit rolled around in her head, keeping her from finding the sleep she needed.

Not wanting to ruin their evening, she'd been hesitant to answer Ernst's question about someone special. Her heart, however, had no problem leaping to an answer.

Ernst must have seen the hesitation on her face, the way she glanced away. Leaning back in his chair, he'd given her an indulgent smile, asking her to be honest. After a moment of vacillating, she felt compelled to tell him the truth.

Taking a deep breath to calm her fluttering stomach, Isabella told Ernst how she'd met a man shortly after arriving in Splendor. They'd become good friends, spending much of their time together, learning a good deal about the other. Their friendship had meant a great deal to her, obviously more than it had to him.

Ernst had seen right through her attempt at indifference. When she'd finished, he'd picked up his coffee, eyeing her over the rim of the glass. Taking a sip, his gaze locked with hers.

"It seems you are in love with Mr. Dixon, Mrs. Boucher. Wouldn't it be easier to speak with the man, admit how you feel?"

Pulling the covers under her chin, Isabella remembered how her jaw had dropped at the mention of Travis's name. She had no idea Ernst knew about him. Her surprise had been so great, she'd never answered his question.

Ernst had been more than gracious. He'd continued their conversation a while longer before thanking her for an enjoyable meal and insightful conversation, then taking her back to Gabe's. He'd helped her from the carriage, escorting her to the door without a hint of disappointment at how their evening had ended.

Staring at the ceiling, she wondered what might have happened if she'd met Ernst first. Closing her eyes, Isabella remembered the one time Travis had kissed her. Not a chaste brush of his lips across her cheek, but an actual kiss.

The feeling of his mouth on hers had stolen her breath, bringing a most unanticipated reaction. She'd loved her husband, been a devoted wife, enjoying the infrequent times he'd come to her bedroom at night. Until Travis,

Isabella hadn't realized what her marriage had lacked. Passion.

Gripping her hands in the covers, Isabella shuddered at what happened next. Travis had stepped away and apologized for his advances, telling her it wouldn't happen again. Even now, a couple months later, her face heated in humiliation.

She'd done her best to push the impact of his kiss from her mind, burying it in some private place in her heart. Travis could never know the effect he had on her or how much she'd wanted him to do it again.

What had been a most glorious event for her apparently had little impact on the man she loved. It hurt, knowing the passion she felt wasn't returned. A few weeks after the kiss, he'd made his announcement, destroying her dreams of any type of life together.

Then he'd shown up tonight.

Yawning, she turned to her side, clutching the sheets under her chin. Perhaps he would attend church tomorrow, sit beside her, and join them for supper. A small ripple of hope raced through her a moment before she drifted off to sleep.

Chapter Seven

Isabella sat next to Lena, forcing herself to stay calm as her gaze searched the church for Travis.

"He'll be here." Lena's confidence far exceeded hers.

"How can you be so sure?" She looked down at the empty place beside her.

"I know Travis. If he's made up his mind he wants something, Baron Klaussner taking you to supper isn't going to stop him." Feeling Jack tug on her arm, Lena looked to her other side. "Yes, sweetheart?"

Jack looked behind him, giving a brief wave. "Can Johann come to the house after services are over, Mama?"

Isabella stilled at Jack's question. If Johann came, Ernst would accompany him. She wasn't quite ready to face him after their conversation at supper the night before.

"We'll see. His father may already have plans for them."

"Can we ask?" Jack kneeled on the bench seat, looking around the church.

Nodding, Lena patted his shoulder. "Yes, we can ask. Now, sit down and please do your best to sit still."

Glancing once more behind her, Isabella's breath caught when she saw Travis walk into the church. Removing his hat, he ran a hand through his hair, his gaze locking on hers. A faint smile crossed his face as he started down the aisle.

"Is this seat taken?"

Pulling her attention from Travis, Isabella sighed, recognizing Albert Payson's voice. "I, um, well...I believe..." She shot another look down the aisle, her heart stilling when Travis shook his head and took an empty seat a few rows back.

Her stomach lurched when she saw who sat next to him. Tabitha Beekman, one of the mail order brides, a beautiful young woman with an easy smile. Isabella winced, seeing her scoot a little closer to Travis, flashing him a brilliant smile.

"Mrs. Boucher?"

Tearing her gaze from Travis and Tabitha, she looked at Albert. "No, the seat isn't taken, Mr. Payson. Please..." She tapped the space beside her.

"It's a beautiful Sunday, don't you think?"

Isabella pushed aside her disappointment, nodding. "Yes, it is."

Clutching her hands together, she inhaled a slow breath, hoping the minister would appear soon. Albert had been a wonderful companion when they'd shared supper and watched the show at Ruby's. As good a time as she had, Isabella didn't intend to see him again, nor did she want to participate in a conversation this morning.

Feeling Lena's hand on her arm, Isabella looked at her friend, unable to keep the pained expression off her face. Lena returned a smug smile.

"I told you Travis would be here."

Nodding, a slight grin appeared on Isabella's face. "So you did." She leaned closer, lowering her voice. "I just wish he wasn't sitting next to Tabitha."

Lena glanced over her shoulder, giving a quick nod when Travis's gaze met hers. "If he had an interest in Tabitha, he wouldn't be staring at you."

Catching her lower lip between her teeth, Isabella felt her face heat. "He is?"

Lena chuckled. "I'm pretty sure he's not looking at me or Albert." The entire church quieted as Reverend Paige entered the sanctuary from a side door. "Don't worry," she whispered. "This is going to work out for you and Travis. I'm quite certain of it."

"Do you have plans for supper, Mrs. Boucher?" Albert walked behind her as they left the church, stepping out into a bright, cloudless sky. Summer in Splendor could bring blistering heat. Today, the moderate temperature signaled a beautiful day.

Isabella cringed. Not from Albert's question, but at the sight of Travis and Tabitha standing several feet away.

"I've made plans with Lena and Gabe." She knew her response sounded sharper than intended. Isabella didn't have it in her to soften her tone. "If you'll excuse me, Mr. Payson."

She glanced once more at Travis, seeing his head tilt back as he laughed at something Tabitha said. Turning away, Isabella searched for Lena, who'd left the church through a side door with Gabe and Jack. Hearing her friend's laughter, she shifted to see Lena talking with one of Gabe's deputies, Cash Coulter, and his wife, Allie.

Refusing to look back at Travis, she moved toward Lena, her footsteps faltering at the sound of gunfire. Before she could figure out where it came from, strong hands pulled her toward the church, then shoved her to the ground when the shots continued.

Heart pounding, Isabella tried to raise her head and dislodge whomever held her down.

"Don't move, Isabella." Travis's forceful voice washed over her.

"What's happening?"

"I don't know."

She felt his weight ease at the same time the firing stopped.

"Come on." Travis helped her up, wrapping his arms around her as he guided her back inside the church, now full of people with confused, scared expressions. "Are you all right?" His gaze wandered over her, searching for wounds.

"I'm fine, Travis."

"Are you sure?" The strain on his face spoke of the depth of his concern.

She nodded. "I'm sure."

He sucked in a breath, giving her a curt nod. "Stay in here. I need to find out what's going on."

Isabella started to follow him. "But—"

"Stay here, Isabella. Please." He bent down, placing a kiss on her cheek, then gestured to those around them. "See if there's anyone who needs your help."

Ignoring her fear, she nodded. "Be careful."

A grim smile curled the corners of his mouth before he hurried to the door. Lifting his gunbelt from a hook, he looked outside then turned back to scan the inside of the church.

Travis searched for Tabitha. He'd left her to find Isabella a few moments before the shots rang out. Finding her huddled in a group inside the church, he switched his attention to anyone who might be injured.

Doc Worthington tended to an older man with an injury to his arm, while Doc McCord wrapped a bandage around the leg of a young boy. Children cried, clutching onto the skirts of their mothers, while men rushed around, seeing who they could help. Gabe, his deputies, Dax, Luke, and other townsfolk huddled near a wagon, strapping guns around their waists and grabbing rifles. Travis did the same, rushing up to them.

"What can I do?"

Gabe turned toward him. "Did you recognize the men who rode past?"

Travis shook his head. "I heard the shots and went for Isabella."

Gabe nodded toward his deputies. "We're going after them. I'd appreciate it if you'd stay here with the Pelletiers and the other men to keep watch over the women and children. Get them all inside the church until we return."

Travis gave a curt nod before walking to where Clay McCord lifted the injured boy into his arms. "I'll take him, Doc. You go ahead and check the others. Gabe wants us to get everyone inside the church."

Handing the boy over, Clay searched the surrounding area. "Have you seen Olivia?"

"Olivia Barnett, Nick's daughter?"

Clay shrugged out of his coat, dropping it to the ground before rolling up his sleeves. "I was talking to her a moment before the shots started. I lost sight of her…" His voice trailed off as he continued to look for her.

"She's probably already in the church, Clay. I'll find her, make sure she's all right." Travis shifted the boy in his arms, taking the steps into the church, the boy's mother right behind them.

"Please. You can put him here." The woman pointed to an empty bench a few feet away.

He laid the boy down, looking for Olivia in the crowded church. "Let me know if you need more help with him."

Sitting next to her son, she touched Travis's arm. "Thank you."

A grim smile crossed his face before he lifted his gaze to search the room. He found Olivia sitting with a few other women, including Isabella. When she looked up, her gaze locked on his, her eyes dark with confusion.

Slipping between those assembled in small groups, he walked over to her. "Gabe and his deputies are searching for the men who shot at us." He looked at those around them. "Did any of you recognize the shooters? Remember anything about them?"

"One was an Indian, Mr. Dixon."

Travis turned to see Jack beside him. He knelt beside the boy. "Are you sure about that?"

Jack's head bobbed up and down. "Yes, sir. He wore a coat and had a rifle, but he had one feather sticking up here." He touched the back of his head. "And he had braids down each side of his face."

"Have you ever seen him before?"

Jack shook his head. "No, Mr. Dixon."

"Did you get a good look at anyone else?"

Jack scrunched his eyes closed, trying to remember. Opening them, his eyes widened. "I saw at least five men on horses. One wore a hat like my papa's." He looked at Lena. "You know, Mama. The old blue one."

Lena nodded. "He means the one Gabe wore during the war, Travis."

Rubbing his chin, Travis tried to think of anyone he knew in Splendor who still wore their Army caps. The last ones were a group of outlaws who'd come after Wyatt. They'd been part of a guerilla group of ex-Confederates who refused to accept the war had ended.

He placed a hand on the boy's shoulder. "Thanks, Jack. You did real good." Standing, he looked at the others. "If you remember anything, let Gabe or one of his deputies know."

Shifting, he spotted Dax, Luke, Bull, and several others standing near doors and windows, weapons ready in case the shooters returned.

Taking off his hat, Travis shredded fingers through his hair, trying to push his anger aside.

"What kind of men shoot into a group of women and children?" Isabella stood next to him, her hand resting on his arm.

"I don't know. We might get some answers when Gabe and the others return."

Isabella looked around, glad the initial panic had turned to frustration and anger. "Someone could've been killed. The boy over there will be lucky if he doesn't lose his leg." Her voice broke on the last.

He'd never seen Isabella lose her temper or cry. Travis studied her, thinking she might be on the brink of both. Putting an arm around her shoulders, he drew her close, placing a kiss on her forehead.

"Gabe will find out who did this, Isabella. From the little I saw, they weren't aiming. Just shooting into those congregated outside. We're real lucky there were just the two wounded."

"Doc!"

Bull's voice rose above the low conversations in the church. Clay walked toward him. "What is it?"

Glancing at Dax and Luke, Bull led the doctor outside. "I found one more victim."

"Show me." Clay started down the steps.

"There's no rush, Doc. He's dead."

Isabella stared at nothing, still shocked at the news. Albert Payson had taken a bullet in the chest, crumbling to the ground not twenty yards from the church.

Sitting in the parlor of Lena's home, she sipped sherry while Gabe, Travis, Wyatt, and Walter talked in the study. Lena and Nora worked in the kitchen, preparing supper with little anticipation the food would get eaten. The announcement of Albert's death pushed many otherwise rational townsfolk to speak of forming a vigilante committee, calling for those responsible to be found and hung.

Gabe had returned in time to calm the most outspoken in the crowd, assuring them those responsible would be found and tried for their crimes. Asking everyone to return home, he and his deputies met with the Pelletiers, Noah, Nick, and several others, before escorting his family home. Travis hadn't considered going back to the ranch until he knew Isabella was all right.

Walter took a sip of whiskey, his face etched with worry. He and Ernst had been talking on one side of the church, protected from the gunfire. Jack and Johann played several yards away, laughing, running around, unprepared for the violence about to come their way.

No one had been prepared for Albert's death.

Gabe rested his hip against the desk, an untouched drink in his hand. "They created chaos, focusing everyone's attention on protecting themselves while they robbed the bank."

Travis nodded, his voice thick with disgust. "They knew most everyone in Splendor attended Sunday services. They also knew most men left their guns outside or in the entry of the church."

"And many don't strap them on until they're ready to ride out," Wyatt added.

Nick looked toward the parlor where his wife, Suzanne, spoke with Isabella. "This wasn't random. They planned the raid."

Wyatt studied the amber liquid in his glass, pinching the bridge of his nose. "Which means we know at least one of them."

"What is Horace going to do?"

Gabe looked at his father. "We have a pretty smart banker in Splendor, although I doubt he'd see it the same way."

Walter finished his drink, setting the glass down. "What do you mean?"

Gabe chuckled, although there was no joy in the sound. "Horace had a bad stomachache Saturday night. He decided to take a walk to the bank, which isn't unusual. I've seen him working well past sunset. He couldn't explain it to me, but something about the amount of money in the main vault bothered him. Horace left less than a quarter of it there, transferring the rest to the hidden vault he had installed last year."

Walter's eyes widened. "I didn't know he had a hidden vault."

"I believe that was Horace's intention, Father. It's best if only a few people know."

Adding more whiskey to his glass, Wyatt paced to the window. "I wish I could be there when the robbers find out they got a small amount of what they'd planned."

Gabe nodded. "That's what worries me. If they expected a lot more, there's no reason they won't come back to get the rest." He walked around his desk, lowering himself into his chair. "They took a well-traveled trail out of town, making it easy to combine their tracks with everyone else's. Cash and Beau are our best trackers. They picked up where the group veered off the trail, then lost them when the outlaws rode into the river. They're going back out in the morning, but I'm guessing those men are camped well away from Splendor."

"Why kill Albert?" Wyatt asked. "He was on his way home."

Gabe shrugged. "Albert may have heard the shooting and turned around. Maybe they thought he might recognize them."

"Hell, they could've done it for pleasure. Men like them don't need much of a reason to kill." Wyatt tossed back the rest of his drink. "So, what do we do now?"

"I'm posting a deputy inside the bank, at least for a few weeks. Horace is going to keep only what money is needed for the next day in the bank. The rest will be placed in the second vault each night. A couple deputies and I will guard him when he makes the transfer. I'll get the word out to keep watch, have guns ready, and be wary of any strangers. Especially those asking questions."

"Nora won't like it, but from now on, I'm wearing my gun inside the church."

Gabe's brows furrowed. "If that's your intention, you'd best let Reverend Paige know, Wyatt. But I agree. It's best we stay armed until we find out who did this."

Walter crossed his arms. "What about the women and children? Those men didn't seem to have any hesitation about shooting into the crowd. It's doubtful they'll hesitate the next time."

Gabe leaned forward, resting his arms on the desk. "Most women know how to shoot and keep a rifle or shotgun with them. I'm thinking if they try again, they'll do the same as the first time."

"Or they'll raid the bank while we're inside the church, not when we're leaving," Travis said.

Wyatt nodded. "It sure makes more sense to do it when no one is around. Sunday was the perfect day for them to catch us unaware."

"I'm going to need every man to be prepared when they come to church. Travis, when you ride back to the ranch, let Dax and Luke know what we've discussed."

"Sure will, Gabe."

"I'm going to send a telegram to the sheriff in Big Pine to let him know what happened." Gabe glanced up to see Lena walking toward him.

"Supper is ready, gentlemen. Are you ready or should we wait a bit?"

Walter stretched his arms above his head. "I don't know about the rest of you, but I'm starving."

Gabe stood, clasping him on the shoulder. "I believe we all agree with you, Father."

Chapter Eight

Travis waited for Isabella while talking with the men in the study. She'd disappeared right after helping in the kitchen after their meal, sending him a quick glance on her way upstairs. They'd spoken little since returning to Gabe's. A few words over supper, nothing of any consequence.

Wyatt and Nora had already left, wanting to get home well before dark. Travis knew he should get back to the ranch, but refused to leave until he knew Isabella's intentions.

"I must ride back to Luke's. Ginny needs my help with Cooper tomorrow."

Hearing Isabella's voice, Travis stood, seeing her and Lena speaking in the entry. She wore a split skirt and velvet riding jacket, her satchel on the floor next to her.

Lena shook her head. "You shouldn't go alone, Isabella. Stay here another night. Gabe can go with you in the morning."

"I'll be riding with her." Travis stepped next to them, prepared to argue if she objected.

Slipping on her gloves, Isabella lifted her gaze to meet his. "Are you sure?"

He cocked his head, giving her a disbelieving look. "I'm not letting you ride out to Luke's alone."

"Don't argue with him, Isabella. If you insist on leaving, you'll need to start soon." Lena looked at Gabe. "Travis is escorting Isabella home."

As the men joined them in the entry, she looked at Travis. "Thank you. I appreciate you going out of your way."

"Isabella, I've never had a problem doing anything for you."

Her brow lifted, but she decided not to respond.

After saying their goodbyes, Travis picked up her satchel. "Are you ready?"

She nodded, giving Lena one more hug before following Travis outside. The sun touched the tops of the western mountains, indicating it would be dark within a couple hours. They had more than enough time to reach Luke's.

Walking into the barn and looking into a nearby stall, a smile crossed his face. Opening the gate, he stepped inside, stroking a hand down the horse's neck. "Blossom. What are you doing here?"

"She's mine, Travis. I bought her from Noah."

He raised a brow. "That's a surprise. Noah told me he planned to save her for Gabriel." Slipping a halter over the mare's head, he led her out of the stall.

"When I explained the horse I wanted, he showed me Blossom. He said she'd be perfect for me."

Picking up a blanket and saddle, he placed them on the mare's back. "Noah was right. She's one of the sweetest horses I've ever trained." He looked at Isabella. "She is perfect for you." Travis handed her the reins before retrieving Banjo from a nearby stall.

"Noah told me you'd trained her."

Travis finished saddling Banjo, then crossed his arms. "I'm surprised you bought a horse I'd worked with."

Her brows furrowed into a frown. "I don't know why. You and Wyatt are the two best trainers around. It would be foolish of me to ignore something as important as that."

Travis stepped to within a foot of her, a solemn expression on his face. "I said some things the last time we spoke..." He glanced away, taking a slow breath.

"It's more what you *didn't* say, Travis." Licking her lips, she pressed on. "You refused to explain why you'd been avoiding me. I'm sure you had your reasons, although I can't pretend it didn't hurt. It still does."

He leaned toward her. "Isabella..." His voice trailed off as he lifted his hand, brushing a finger down her cheek.

She turned her face, tightening her grip on Blossom's reins. "You can't force yourself to care about someone. I know that as well as anyone. My husband was a wonderful man. Kind, generous, and truthful. As you know, he was a good deal older than me...my father's age. Still, I grew to care for him a great deal." Isabella's sad gaze locked on his. "I'll not settle for anything less than love again. Your friendship has meant a great deal to me. More than you know. The problem is I've grown to love you. As hard as it is to accept, I realize you'll never see me as more than a friend." She started leading Blossom outside.

"Isabella, wait." When she didn't stop, he rushed to grab her arm. "You're wrong."

"I don't need you to explain why, Travis. Can't we please let it be?" When she lifted her face, he winced at her haunted expression.

"No, we can't leave it be."

Wrapping his arm around her waist, Travis pulled her to him. Taking a moment to stare at the tenderness on her face, he lowered his mouth to hers.

A sense of urgency claimed him as he deepened the kiss. His tongue traced the fullness of her lips before exploring the recesses of her mouth. Hearing a ragged sigh escape her, Travis crushed her to him. A heat he'd never felt, not even with his wife, rushed through his body.

Feeling her squirm against him, he raised his head, gazing into her eyes. He did his best to hide the satisfaction he felt at the dazed look on her face.

Travis stepped back, watching as she touched a finger to her swollen lips.

"Now you know how much I care about you, Isabella."

She shook her head, confusion contorting her features. "I thought..." Swallowing the contradiction claiming her, she glanced away.

"I can't promise this is love, Isabella. What I can promise is I care a great deal about you."

Staring at the torment on his face, she placed a hand against his chest. "You're still in love with your wife, Travis. It's hard to admit, but you might never be able to love anyone in the same way."

A muscle worked in his jaw as he drew in a deep breath. "I don't know what to think. You're the only woman who stirs any feelings in me. Maybe it is love."

"And maybe it isn't. We've both been married, know what it's like to be with another person. It's normal to want to feel that closeness with someone else. It doesn't mean you love the person."

He snorted, taking her hand in his. "Does that mean you could make love to me without loving me?"

She shook her head. "No, it doesn't. I believe it's different with men. You wanting me, needing to be with me, has little to do with being in love."

Isabella's comment stayed with Travis all the way to Luke's house, where she'd let him kiss her goodnight before he rode to Dax's. He couldn't stop wondering if his feelings sprang from lust or if love drove him to be with her. After being married to a wonderful woman, he should know the difference.

The confusion came when he thought of the two women at the same time. Two people couldn't be more different. His wife came from a family of farmers, worked alongside him in the fields and with the horses, and knew how to protect herself and their daughter from intruders. Of average height and very slim, she wore her dark blonde hair tucked under a wide-brimmed hat, strands always escaping to brush across her face. Her skin had a warm glow from working long hours in the sun.

Isabella couldn't be more than five-foot-five. She kept her dark brown hair tucked into a neat bun. She may not have grown up with money, but while married to her husband, had become accustomed to the finer side of life. Her refined speech and excellent taste testified to a woman of wealth. An odd set of characteristics given the generosity of her heart and beauty in her soul. She also had more curves than his wife. A body men noticed when she walked past.

Travis found his body hardening, remembering how she felt in his arms a few hours earlier. Although he lusted after her, he also knew his feelings were much more than desire or friendship. Were they love? Travis hoped it wouldn't be long before he knew for certain.

Laramie, Wyoming

"Do you need help with your bag, Mr. Peeler?" The conductor hovered over him, eyeing David's satchel.

He tightened his grip on the handles, shaking his head. "No, thank you."

David looked out the grimy window, cringing at the dust swirling around everyone. The once quiet frontier town had grown since the railroad built the tracks on the outskirts. Some people moved on, heading toward the Pacific. For others, it was the last stop before taking a stagecoach or horse to their next destination.

Stepping onto the platform, David looked for a sign pointing him toward a stagecoach.

"Help you with somethin'?"

The sight of a man in a buckskin jacket and fur cap had him taking a step backward. It wasn't just the idea of someone wearing such heavy clothing in the middle of summer that had him gawking. The man stood at least six-foot-six with a ruddy complexion and scraggly beard reaching down to his chest. Not the sort of person David encountered on the streets of Philadelphia.

Clearing his throat, he nodded. "Where would I find a stagecoach?"

The man studied his face, then tilted his head to the side. "You lookin' to take the stage today, or are you fixin' to stay a spell in Laramie before movin' on?"

"I'd like to leave as soon as possible."

"Where you travelin'?"

"North," David answered, his gaze darting around.

"Then follow me."

Holding the satchel against his chest, David saw others looking at them, acknowledging the tall man beside him. Walking around the building, they stepped onto the main street. David spotted a stagecoach twenty yards away.

"The stage in front of us leaves for Big Pine in an hour. That's in the Montana Territory."

"It is close to Splendor?"

The man nodded. "It'll go there after Big Pine. The office is in the buildin'. That's where you'll pay for a ticket."

Reaching into his pocket, David extracted a coin, holding it out to the man.

"I ain't no hotel porter. Keep your money." Turning away, the man took brisk steps, mumbling under his breath.

Staring after him, David slipped the coin back into his pocket. By the time the train stopped in St. Louis, he'd figured out this would be much more than an escape from his past. The trip would be an adventure he wasn't quite convinced he wanted to make.

As if I have a choice in the matter. David shook his head on the thought, stepping onto the boardwalk and inside the stagecoach station.

"Yes, sir. What can I do for you?"

Setting the satchel on the counter, David reached into a pocket. "I need to go to Splendor."

The clerk nodded. "Montana Territory, huh?" He quoted him a price. "You've got an hour to grab some food before the stage leaves. Don't expect much at any of the stops. If you want a suggestion, you'll get a hotel room in Big Pine.

Take a bath, eat a good meal, then leave for Splendor the next morning."

"I'm in a hurry to reach Splendor."

Chuckling, the clerk shook his head. "Won't matter. The stage stays overnight in Big Pine."

Snorting, David nodded. "Understood. Can you direct me to a nearby restaurant?"

"Right next door. Good food and they won't rob you like some of the new places that sprung up after the railroad decided to stop here."

David lifted the satchel. "Thank you."

"Just be back here in an hour. The stage doesn't wait, and I don't give refunds."

Giving a tight nod, David covered the distance between the stage office and restaurant in less than a minute, taking the only empty table in the place. Ordering the special, he set his bag on the chair beside him, glancing around the room. His gaze locked on a man in the opposite corner, his head buried in a newspaper.

David's chest tightened. The same man from Philadelphia who'd spoken to him in Omaha. The same man who hadn't given David his name.

He told himself it could be a coincidence. Hearing the train whistle, looking out the window to see it pulling away from the station, David's gut twisted. He'd never believed in coincidences.

Isabella held Abby's hand as they stood outside the room in the clinic used for burial preparation. Both were still working through the shock of Albert's violent death. A decent, kind man, he deserved better.

Abby had sent a telegram to Albert's brother in Boston, notifying him of his death. Today being Monday, Abby knew Ernie wouldn't be able to attend the funeral on Tuesday.

Ernie opened the law office in Splendor to help her with a complicated estate after her father died. Not long after Albert traveled west to join him in the practice, Ernie decided to return to Boston. Albert had done an excellent job earning the trust of the townsfolk. His tragic death was a terrible blow to the growing town. Everyone hoped Ernie would move back and keep the practice going, or at least arrange for another attorney to take over.

Isabella had felt the need to come by and pay her respects in private, before the public services. It saddened her knowing Albert had no one of consequence in Splendor. She liked him, enjoyed his quiet, subtle jokes, and would miss seeing him in town.

"Will Noah be providing the wagon to take Albert to the cemetery?"

Abby nodded, letting out a ragged breath. "Yes. After Reverend Paige finishes the funeral at the church, Noah will deliver the body. He has a couple men preparing the grave today." She swiped a tear from her cheek. "Such a senseless killing. I swear, I just don't understand some people."

"Nobody understands the mind of a killer, Abby. The men who killed Albert are nothing more than brutal murderers, caring nothing for anyone except themselves. I doubt they even care much about each other. My hope is Gabe finds them."

Nodding, Abby squeezed Isabella's hand before letting go. "You're right. After all that's happened in Splendor, I should be used to the irrational violence."

"I doubt anyone could ever get used to what happened yesterday. This could've happened anywhere. All we can do is protect ourselves and not make ourselves targets. The outlaws knew the men wouldn't have their guns with them during church. Gabe and Travis think they'll try the same thing again."

"Go after the bank when no one is armed and can stop them," Abby whispered.

Isabella nodded. "My understanding is the men will be keeping their guns with them in church. At least until the outlaws are caught."

"I think it's a good idea. In fact, I plan to keep mine with me all the time. You should do the same, Isabella. There's no reason we women can't protect the town the same way as the men."

Nodding, she chuckled. "When Travis escorted me home yesterday, he mentioned giving me lessons." A slight grin split her face. "We're to have the first one on Saturday."

"An excellent idea. Maybe I can get Noah to do the same with some of the women in town who know nothing about protecting themselves. He can start with the mail order brides."

Isabella bit her lip, her gaze locked in concentration. "Perhaps we could all get together at one time. It would be so much better to learn with other women."

Abby slipped her arm through Isabella's. "I'll speak with Noah and you can talk to Travis. I'm sure they'll both be happy to help us."

Noah's fork stopped midway to his mouth as he stared at his wife in disbelief. "You want Travis and me to teach a dozen women to use a gun?"

Abby nodded. "All at the same time, of course. That way, you and Travis won't have to give up too much work or free time."

"Abby?" Setting down his fork, he rested his arms on the table.

She helped Gabriel scoop some potatoes into his mouth. "Hmmm?"

"Have any of these women ever held a gun before?"

Turning back to Noah, she shrugged. "A couple...maybe. Does it matter?"

He shook his head, frustration showing in the set of his jaw. "If they learned, do you think they would have the courage to shoot if needed?"

Abby sat back in her chair, her mouth twisting. "I can't answer that, Noah. Until my life depended on it, I wasn't certain I could kill someone. And I'd do it again if it meant protecting someone or saving my life. My guess is no one knows until they're faced with those decisions."

Picking up his coffee, Noah took a sip. "Which women are you talking about?"

"Well, I'll be there and so will Isabella. Nora and Allie want to join us, as do the mail order brides. Lena is a good shot, but I think she would want to come along. Sarah Murton wants to learn, and so does Mrs. Paige."

His brows shot up. "The reverend's wife?"

"Why not? The shooting took place right outside the church. She was extremely angry about the entire event and is calling for the women to meet and discuss how to defend ourselves."

Shaking his head, Noah rubbed his palms against his eyes. "All right. I'll talk to Travis."

Standing, Abby wrapped her arms around his neck and kissed him. "Thank you so much. You won't regret this."

Chapter Nine

The morning of Albert's funeral brought dark clouds and brisk winds. Just after noon, the skies opened, blanketing the town with a constant drizzle. The weather didn't stop people from crowding into the church to honor a young man who died too soon.

Travis rode into town with the Pelletiers, taking a seat next to Isabella. Reaching over, he covered her hand with his, giving it a light squeeze. He leaned toward her.

"Are you doing all right?"

She nodded, her mouth drawing into a thin line. "I'm fine."

"I know Albert meant something to you." Travis wished he'd stayed silent when he saw her eyes widen.

"I'm not sure what you mean."

The music slowed, then stopped, signaling the start of the service and saving Travis from replying. Isabella would remember his comment and want an explanation. He had no intention of lying to her, even if it meant provoking her anger.

She leaned close, whispering in his ear as Reverend Paige began. "We'll talk after the service."

Nodding, Travis squeezed her hand again, doing his best to listen to the eulogy and not think about the woman beside him. He'd left her at Luke's house Sunday night with a promise—never again would he shut her out. No matter his doubts about being able to fully commit to a future together, Travis wanted her in his life.

When Reverend Paige finished, the music started again. Filing out of the church, people spoke in low whispers, the mood somber as they prepared for the short trip to the cemetery. At least the rain had stopped. A small consolation on a sad occasion.

Isabella glanced up at him. "Tie Banjo to the back of Gabe's buggy and ride with us."

Travis did as she asked, sitting next to her as Gabe drove them to the cemetery. Most ranchers and farmers had small plots for family on their property, while the cemetery mainly held those with little or no land. Most of those living in town would end up in the beautiful grassland tended by church women.

Gabe glanced over his shoulder at Travis as he pulled the buggy to a stop. "Beau and Cash found the remains of a camp a few miles from town."

"How old?"

"They're guessing a day at most. From the looks of it, there must've been six to eight riders."

Setting the brake, Gabe jumped to the ground then helped Lena down.

Travis did the same for Isabella, catching her hand when he set her on the soaked ground. Looking behind them, he saw Noah, a coffin in the back of his wagon.

He wanted to ask Gabe more questions about what Cash and Beau found, but kept silent. There'd be time after they laid Albert to rest.

Leaving Isabella with Lena and Jack, Travis helped Gabe, Noah, and a few others with the coffin. Lowering it into the already prepared grave, the men stepped away.

The graveside service took little time. A few children tossed flowers on top of the coffin before Reverend Paige led them in a final prayer. When everyone began to disperse, Isabella stepped forward, staring down, swiping a tear from her cheek.

"I'm sorry about what happened to Albert. He seemed like a good man."

She glanced at Travis, giving him a slow nod. "He was." She reached out, threading her fingers through his. "You said something earlier about him meaning something to me."

He shook his head. "We'd best get back to the wagon. I don't want to hold Gabe up."

Shaking her head, Isabella refused to budge. "Not yet. Tell me what you meant."

Looking away, he let out a slow breath before turning back. "I saw the two of you one night."

"You did?"

Travis nodded. "The boys and I were in town for supper and decided to go to Ruby's. You and Albert were at a table near the stage. The way you looked at each other, I thought, well...it appeared you had feelings for each other."

Tightening her grip on his hand, she shook her head. "Albert and I went to supper once. He offered to escort me to Ruby's, and I accepted."

"You must've cared about him or you wouldn't have accepted."

Dropping her hand from his, she crossed her arms. "I liked him, Travis. Beyond that, what I felt or didn't feel for Albert isn't your concern. You made it clear you had no interest in being more than a friend."

"I never said that, Isabella," he ground out, his jaw hardening.

Glaring at him, she took a step closer. "You didn't have to. It was obvious by the way you avoided me, then made some ridiculous excuse for not riding out to Luke's to visit." Looking behind him, she saw Gabe, Lena, and Jack waiting in the buggy. "We need to go." She began to move past him, stopping when he grabbed her arm.

"Not yet."

Tugging her arm free, Isabella glared up at him. "Albert asked me to supper and I went. Baron Klaussner asked me to supper and I went with him, too." She placed fisted hands on her hips. "Does it surprise you that other men would ask me out?"

Clenching his hands at his sides, he stared at her. "Yes. I mean, no. Ah, hell..." Travis scrubbed a hand down his face, taking a few steps away. He'd never meant to argue with her. Worse, he didn't understand why he felt so angry. He already knew about Albert and Ernst. Closing his eyes, he sucked in a deep breath, stilling when he felt Isabella's hand on his shoulder.

"Why does who took me to supper bother you, Travis? We're friends. Aren't we?"

He shook his head, turning to look at her. "We're much more than friends, Isabella."

"Are you two all right?" Gabe stood a few yards away, concern etched in his features.

Travis nodded. "We're fine, Gabe." He looked at Isabella. "We'd better get going." Holding out his arm, he waited until she slipped hers through it.

Following Gabe to the buggy, Travis thought about what he'd admitted, wondering if Isabella felt the same confusion as him. By the look on her face, she did.

Noah and Travis stood at the back of the wagon, sorting ammunition and guns, giving each other furtive looks.

"Tell me again how we got into this."

Noah raised a brow. "As I recall, you offered to teach Isabella how to shoot."

Travis snorted, glancing over his shoulder. "Isabella, not a passel of females."

Chuckling, Noah shook his head. "Too late to back out now, my friend."

Ten women stood several yards away, excitement obvious by their animated discussions and the way they kept casting quick glances at the men.

Four days after the funeral, Travis still hadn't spoken to Isabella about what he'd said before leaving the cemetery. Albert's death had caused his work at the ranch to stall, forcing him and Wyatt to work long days in order to fulfill the existing contract. Wyatt didn't ride home to Nora until late Friday night. Travis was able to get a message to Isabella through Luke, letting her know he still planned to work with the women on Saturday. When she arrived, they'd said a brief hello before she joined the other women, leaving him to work with Noah.

"Are you ready?" Noah picked up a six-shooter and box of ammunition.

Travis nodded. "What do you suggest?"

"You take five and I'll take five."

"I'm guessing you want Abby in your group."

Noah looked at him as if he'd lost his mind. "Hell no. I don't want her angry with me tonight. To start, you take my wife and I'll take Isabella. After an hour, we'll change groups."

"I sure hope I'm as good at this as you."

Noah snickered, his eyes dancing with mischief as they walked toward the ladies. "You're a Johnny Reb, my friend. You'll never be as good as me."

Travis waited for the sting of remorse to slice through him, surprised when he felt his mouth turn up into a grin. "We'll see about that, Billy Yank."

"Good morning, ladies." Noah looked over the group, his gaze landing on Abby. "We understand you're here because you want to learn to handle a gun and use it for protection." Several nodded, a couple answering in the affirmative. "Good. You know what happened last Sunday. Those outlaws caught us unprepared. They aren't going to do that again."

Travis stepped forward. "Noah and I are going to split you into two groups. After an hour, we'll switch so each of you has a chance to work with both of us. Are any of you proficient with a six-shooter?"

Lena and Abby held up their hands.

"Two of you. Do any of you have experience with a rifle or shotgun?"

Deborah Chestro and Sylvia Lucero, two of the mail order brides, raised their hands, along with Lena and Abby.

"Allie Coulter, I know you can shoot a shotgun." Noah smiled at her.

"I can, but nothing like Lena and Abby."

Noah nodded, looking at Travis. "We'll start with six-shooters. If there's time, we'll work with rifles and shotguns. Noah will start with you five." Travis pointed to five of the women, including Isabella. "The rest of you will come with me."

They'd picked a large clearing not far from town. Several yards into the center, Noah and Travis had set up two rows of targets, one for each group. Additional targets lay a few feet away.

Travis looked over his shoulder to see five solemn-faced women following him in a single line—Abby, Deborah, May, Lena, and Sarah Murton, the town school teacher. Two who already knew how to use a gun and three who didn't.

This shouldn't be too hard, Travis thought.

An hour later, Travis scratched his head. Abby and Lena did well, stepping aside after a few minutes to allow him more time with Deborah, May, and Sarah. Deborah did better than he expected, hitting several targets after missing the first five shots. May didn't do quite as well. It took her sixteen tries to nick one target.

"Did you see that, Mr. Dixon?" she squealed. "I hit it." Turning toward him, she jumped up and down, dropping the gun, screaming at the accidental discharge.

"For the love of..." Travis leaned down, picking up the six-shooter. "Is everyone all right?" When everyone nodded, he turned back to May. "Miss Bacon, you did real good hitting the target. From now on, *never* lose control of your gun. No matter how excited you become, you can't allow yourself to forget this is a dangerous weapon." Ignoring the tears forming in her eyes, he continued. "Someone could've gotten seriously hurt. Do you understand what I'm saying?"

Biting her lower lip, she nodded. "Yes, Mr. Dixon. I'll be real careful from now on."

"Good." He offered her the gun. "Now, try again."

She'd fired three more times, hitting the target on the last shot. This time, she stayed calm, her grip remaining firm.

Travis began to feel a little smug at the ladies' progress. Then Sarah stepped forward.

He could see her tremble from several feet away. "Are you all right, Miss Murton?"

Nodding, she stared at the gun in his hand. "I'll be fine, Mr. Dixon." She lifted her hand to take the gun he held out. Travis couldn't miss the way it shook.

"You don't have to do this, Miss Murton. If you aren't comfortable—"

"No, Mr. Dixon. I want to do this. I *will* do this." She squared her shoulders, determination etched on her face. "I'll not let my students down by not being able to protect them. Now, show me what to do."

"As long as you're sure."

She gave him a curt nod. "I am."

A rocky start became a lesson in persistence. Soft-spoken, somewhat timid, Miss Murton found her courage, listening to everything Travis told her. After six misses, she hit three targets in a row. Instead of showing the elation May had, Sarah let out a relieved breath, lifting her chin.

"I'll need more practice, but I do think I'm getting the idea."

Chuckling, Travis nodded, taking the gun she held out to him. "You're right on both, Miss Murton."

The women took one more turn before Travis and Noah changed groups. Before Travis had a chance to talk with Isabella, Tabitha hurried up to him, slipping an arm through his.

"I'm so glad you offered to teach us, Mr. Dixon."

He glanced behind her at Isabella, wincing at the amused look on her face. "It was Isabella's idea to include all of you, Miss Beekman, not mine."

"Really? She's such a quiet woman. I never would've thought of Mrs. Boucher as someone with such a progressive attitude about women." She slowly turned them around, walking to where Travis's group would be shooting.

His brows furrowed. "Excuse me?"

"Well, the men back home want to keep women safe in the home, ignoring the fact danger can happen anywhere. People in Splendor are so much more open to women learning skills besides cooking, sewing, and gardening. Did your wife know how to shoot, Mr. Dixon?"

Coming to an abrupt halt, a muscle in his jaw ticked as he dropped his arm to his side. "How do you know about my wife?"

Tabitha blanched. "I'm sorry. I didn't mean to anger you."

"What do you know about my wife, Miss Beekman?"

She glanced around, clearing her throat. "Only that she and your daughter died during the war, nothing more. I'm so sorry for saying anything, Mr. Dixon. I sometimes speak before thinking. Please, forgive me."

Shaking off the bleak image of crosses marking two graves in Tennessee, Travis looked at her. "It's all right, Miss Beekman. To answer your question, yes, my wife was a very good shot. Her father taught her, the same as my father taught me."

"Are you two all right?" Isabella stepped next to them, placing a hand on Travis's arm.

Lifting her chin, Tabitha met Isabella's gaze. "We're fine, Mrs. Boucher."

Without thought, Travis placed an arm around Isabella's shoulders, leaning down to kiss her cheek. "Are you ready for your next lesson, sweetheart?"

Neither heard Tabitha's quiet gasp or noticed the stunned look on her face, their attention riveted on each other.

"I am. Noah is such a wonderful teacher."

"Hmm. Sounds like a challenge."

She patted his arm, her lips tilting up into an impish grin. "I find everything is a challenge with you, Mr. Dixon."

Chapter Ten

David stepped from the stagecoach, setting the satchel on the boardwalk before swiping layers of dust from his clothes. The dirt flew off in large plumes, causing him to cough. Removing a handkerchief from an inside pocket, he wiped his hands as he looked around.

The trip through Montana was brutal. None of the five passengers had been prepared for the deep ruts bouncing the stage around as if it weighed nothing. More than once, they'd tumbled into each other or knocked their heads on the roof of the coach. Bruised and battered didn't begin to describe how David's body felt as he bent to grab his bag, then looked at the stagecoach driver.

"Do you have a recommendation where I might find accommodations?"

"The St. James Hotel is down the street. It's the finest hotel in all of Montana. The boardinghouse is right there." He pointed across the crowded street. "It's run by a woman named Suzanne Barnett. Clean rooms, assuming she has one available, and her restaurant is open to anyone."

"Would you happen to know Mrs. Isabella Boucher?"

The driver scratched his stubbled chin, then shook his head. "Can't say as I do. Mrs. Barnett or the sheriff would know. The jail is just up the street."

"Thank you." David crossed the street toward the boardinghouse. He'd eat a meal and discover if anyone knew Isabella.

Before reaching the front door, he saw a large group enter town. A few women sat in a wagon while others flanked them on horseback. Laughter filled the air as they rode past to stop in front of the livery.

David took a few steps forward, stopping at the edge of the boardwalk. Keeping his bag tucked against his chest, he watched a tall, slender man dismount, then help a woman with dark brown hair slide down from her horse. He placed a kiss on her cheek, then turned to speak to the other man in the group. At the same time, the woman shifted, glancing in David's direction.

His pulse quickened. He'd traveled over two thousand miles to find the woman he sought. The woman he planned to marry. Raising his hand, he stepped onto the street.

"Isabella!" David waved as he hurried toward her. Seeing her gaze lock on his, he waved again. "Isabella!"

A bright smile lit her face. "David!" She took a few steps forward, unaware of Travis watching from a few feet away.

Stopping in front of her, David set the satchel on the ground, wrapping her in a hug, which appeared decidedly familiar to Travis. Crossing his arms, he watched as she kissed David's cheek, her hands gripping the man's arms.

"What a wonderful surprise. What are you doing here?" Dropping her arms, she stepped away.

"I'm here for you, Isabella."

Her brows furrowed. "For me?"

He nodded, bending to pick up his bag. "As I promised Arnott before he died."

She shook her head, clasping her hands together. "What promise, David?"

Giving her an indulgent look, he reached out, placing a hand on her shoulder. "I thought he told you. Arnott made me promise to take care of you after his death." He inched closer. "He insisted on it, Isabella."

"What?"

Travis watched her face flush, hands clenched at her sides. He stepped closer, taking her elbow. "I'd suggest we go to the Eagle's Nest so your friend here can explain what he means."

"I don't know who you are, but this is a private conversation between Isabella and me."

Travis lifted a brow, his lips twisting into a sardonic grin. "You may join us or not, Mr..."

David glanced at Isabella, noticing her lean into the man's side. "Peeler. David Peeler."

Travis held out his hand. "Travis Dixon."

A moment passed as David stared at the outstretched hand. Making a decision, he grasped it, then pulled his hand away, looking at Isabella.

"I'd prefer to speak with you alone."

"Whatever you have to say can be said in front of Travis. He's a good friend."

"A very good friend, Mr. Peeler," Travis added.

David couldn't hide his shocked expression as he looked between the two. "You don't mean..." His voice trailed off, his face paling.

"Travis and I are quite close, David, and he's right. We should get a table at the Eagle's Nest, where we may speak with more privacy." She slipped her arm through Travis's. "Are we agreed?"

David glared at Travis before giving Isabella a terse nod. "Fine. I shall follow you."

Isabella stared across the table at David, back rigid as she tapped the cup of tea with her fingers. "I want to know exactly what Arnott said to you."

David's hand shook as he picked up his coffee and took a sip. Setting it down, he pulled a handkerchief from his pocket, blotting his forehead. Clearing his throat, he opened his mouth to speak, letting out a relieved breath when the waiter appeared.

"Are you ready to order, Mrs. Boucher?"

She gave the older man a warm smile. "I am, Oscar. I'd like the soup and corned beef."

"Excellent choice, Mrs. Boucher. Mr. Dixon?"

"The corned beef and cooked cabbage, Oscar."

"Wonderful." He looked at David. "And you, sir?"

Scanning the menu once more, he wrinkled his nose. "Chicken."

"With potatoes, sir?"

"Of course." Handing Oscar the menu, David met Isabella's unwavering gaze.

"I believe you were about to tell me about the promise you made to Arnott."

David nodded, ignoring the way Travis leaned forward. "His wishes were quite clear. He made me promise to take care of you after his death. Make certain you were safe from those who might take advantage." He shot Travis a scornful glance. "Arnott knew you and I had a special friendship. A bond, if you will. Do you not agree?"

Her features softened a little. "You and I have been friends since my marriage. You helped me ease into Philadelphia society, for which I will always be grateful."

"This was Arnott's point. For many reasons, he believed you and I would be well suited."

Isabella's brows furrowed. "Well suited for what?"

"Marriage, of course."

Eyes sparking, her mouth gaped open, a deep flush creeping up her face. "Marriage? You must be mistaken. Or insane."

"I assure you, I am neither. Arnott felt our backgrounds, education, social status, as well as our mutual desire to marry and have a family, made us a good match. All of these reasons are why he made me promise we'd marry after his death."

She shook her head, her hands fisting in her lap. "Arnott has been gone a long time, David. Much too long to believe you took the promise seriously."

"I can understand your concern, Isabella. Unfortunately, you left Philadelphia quite unexpectedly. It took me a good deal of time to put my affairs in order and travel west."

Her brows wrinkled, voice rising. "You and I have been corresponding for months. Not once did you mention your conversation with Arnott."

He offered an uneasy chuckle. "It isn't the type of thing you mention in a letter, Isabella. I came here to speak to you of his wishes. I must say, Arnott was quite forceful about what he wanted."

"Here you are." Oscar set down a tray holding their food, halting the conversation. Setting plates before them, he stepped back. "May I get you anything else?"

"This will be fine, Oscar. Thank you." Travis's attention switched to Isabella, who'd said nothing after hearing what David stated were Arnott's wishes. He'd felt certain she'd dispute David, deny her late husband would ever make such a statement without speaking with her. The longer she stayed silent, the more uncertain Travis became.

Perhaps she did believe Arnott had made such a request. Or worse, maybe she already knew his wishes, traveling to Splendor to avoid such a union. At this point, Travis didn't know what to think.

Isabella's mind reeled. Arnott had been twenty-five years older than her, yet they'd shared everything. They'd spoken of her future after his death, how he'd reached an agreement with their banker to work with her on his estate. Arnott assured her she'd never have to worry about money. At the time, Isabella hadn't cared about the finances as much as wanting to see her husband recover. He hadn't.

And not once had he mentioned confiding his wishes to David. Isabella had no doubt Arnott wouldn't have kept something so important from her.

Picking up her fork, she stabbed a piece of corned beef, lifting it to her mouth, then setting it back onto her plate.

"I'm sorry, David, but none of what you say makes sense to me." She sucked in an angry breath, her gaze moving over the other diners before returning to David.

Reaching into a pocket, he pulled out an envelope. Opening it, he lifted a somewhat crumpled piece of paper, handing it to her. "Perhaps this will help."

Taking it from him, she read the handwritten message, the style reminding her of Arnott's pen. Her bottom lip trembled, as did her hand, the meaning becoming clear. Looking up, she shook her head.

"I don't understand any of this. Arnott would've told me his thoughts about a union before speaking with you, David. He never would've committed me to such an outrageous action."

Travis reached out. "May I?" Taking it from her shaky hand, he scanned it quickly, his jaw hardening. "Is this your late husband's writing?"

David shot him a frustrated glare. "I assure you it is."

Ignoring him, Travis focused on Isabella. "Is this his writing?"

Biting her lower lip, she shook her head. "I'm not certain. It could be."

"Of course it's his writing. I didn't travel across the country to this uncivilized town on a whim, Isabella. I came here to fulfill Arnott's dying wish." David scooped up a bit of chicken.

She cocked her head at him. "When did he write this?"

His fork stopped midway to his mouth. "The night before he died."

She thought of Arnott's last hours, trying to remember who visited and if David had been at the house. Shaking her head, she rested her clasped hands on the edge of the table.

"I don't recall you being at the house in the days before his death."

David attempted to set a hand on hers, stopping when she pulled them away. "You were quite distraught during the final days of his illness. No one would blame you if you didn't recall all of those who visited."

Her gaze hardened on his. "I'm certain I'd remember you being there, David. He thought of you as a younger brother, a part of the family. No matter how *distraught* I was, I'd remember your presence."

An indulgent expression appeared on his face, his voice softening. "Regardless, I was there the night before he passed. As I recall, you were talking to your banker in the study when Arnott spoke of his desires and gave me the letter." He nodded at the paper Travis still held in his hand. "I don't know why he never mentioned it to you as he'd obviously given it a great deal of thought."

Pressing a finger to her temple, she closed her eyes, doing her best to remember who'd been in the house the days prior to Arnott's death. Isabella recalled meeting with their banker the evening before her husband died. To her knowledge, except for their servants, no one else had been in the house. Opening her eyes, Isabella looked at her full plate, feeling none of the hunger she had before David's surprise declaration.

"Travis, would you mind accompanying me home?"

"Not at all." Folding the letter, Travis stood, glancing at David's outstretched hand. "Since Arnott's note was addressed to Isabella, I believe it is hers to keep." Ignoring the anger building on David's face, he stepped behind Isabella's chair, pulling it out. "We'll leave whenever you're ready."

"I'm ready now." She looked at David. "Thank you for delivering the message. I'm sure you'll understand if I'm skeptical of the contents."

Nodding, he stood, stepping beside her. "Of course. Still, your doubts don't invalidate Arnott's wishes. Don't forget. You owe him a great deal, Isabella."

Lifting her chin, she stared at him. "No one needs to remind me how much I owe Arnott. Without him, well..." Isabella's voice trailed off, her chest squeezing at what would've become of her if she hadn't met Arnott. Taking a deep breath, she exhaled, moving closer to Travis. "I'll still not rush into anything. Where will you be staying?"

"I'd hoped to stay with you."

Travis took a step forward, silencing Isabella's response. "That's out of the question, Mr. Peeler. Isabella lives on a ranch, acting as a nanny."

David blinked a couple times before his wide eyes settled on Isabella's. "Surely he's jesting. Why would a woman such as you stoop to being a nanny for another family?"

"The reasons are mine alone, David. Now, if you'll excuse me." She slipped her arm through Travis's.

"Wait. How will I reach you?"

Travis leaned down, his face a few inches from David's. "Give a message to Sheriff Evans. He'll make sure it reaches Isabella."

Stepping into the afternoon sun, Isabella sucked in a deep breath, letting the warm air fill her lungs. She gripped Travis's arm, his steady presence giving her strength. He leaned down, kissing her temple.

"I want to talk to Gabe and let him know about David."

"You know he'll be able to find me, Travis. Everyone in town knows I live with Luke and Ginny."

"That's one reason I want to speak with Gabe. A few words from him may warn David away from riding out to speak with you."

They walked across the street to the jail. Glancing over her shoulder, Isabella spotted David standing on the steps of the St. James. "I know David, and he won't let this rest. He'll continue to pursue this, pushing for a decision."

Stopping outside the jail, he turned her toward him. "You don't believe what he's saying, do you?"

Looking away, she thought of Arnott, how he'd changed her life by offering marriage. "You never met Arnott, Travis. He never thought of himself as most in his position do. It wouldn't surprise me if he did consider who I might marry after his death." She shifted to look up at him. "My husband always wanted what was best for me. If what David says is true, I must at least consider Arnott's wishes."

His hand tightened on her arm, his stormy eyes meeting hers. "Do you love him?"

The air left her lungs, her features softening. "You know I don't."

"But you'd sacrifice your own desires for what you think your dead husband would want?"

"You don't understand, Travis."

"Then help me understand why you'd even consider marrying a man you don't love, haven't seen in years, when you have a man standing in front of you who'd..." The rest of what he'd meant to say died on his lips when the door of the jail opened.

"I thought I heard Travis's voice out here." Gabe stepped outside, feeling the tension between the two. "Did I interrupt something?"

Pinching the bridge of his nose, Travis shook his head. "No. We were coming to see you."

"I've got some time before I have to ride out to meet Luke. Come on inside." He moved aside, letting them walk in. "Sit down."

"I know Luke came to town yesterday. Is there something going on at the ranch?" Isabella asked, taking a seat.

Gabe shook his head. "I'm not sure. A few missing cattle, mainly from the northern border of the ranch. It could be the Crow are raiding again."

"They'd be darn close to the Blackfoot territory," Travis said.

Gabe nodded. "Luke feels the same. He just wants me to ride out and take a look. It's doubtful I'll find anything. So, why did you want to talk to me?"

It didn't take long for Travis and Isabella to describe David's unannounced arrival in Splendor and her desire to keep where she lived from him. Neither mentioned the letter, nor the strain it caused between them.

"I'll keep watch on Mr. Peeler and caution him away from trying to find you, Isabella. With everyone in town knowing where you live, I'd suggest you prepare for him to show up. There's no law against Peeler riding out to Luke's."

A grim smile formed on Isabella's face. "I just need time to consider what we discussed, Gabe. Whatever you can do is appreciated."

"You know I'll do anything possible for you, Isabella. I'd best get out to see Luke."

"May I ride with you, Gabe?"

"It'd be my pleasure."

Travis's head snapped toward her, deep furrows between his eyes.

The smile she offered didn't show in her eyes. "There's no reason for you to go out of your way when Gabe is heading there anyway."

"It's not out of my way," Travis ground out, too low for Gabe to hear. Standing, he helped her up.

She didn't respond, following Gabe outside and walking to the livery. Travis stayed beside her, trying to figure out what he'd said to push her away. Stopping outside Noah's shop, she turned toward him.

"Will you be at church tomorrow?"

Glancing away, Travis settled fisted hands on his hips. "If you'll save me a place next to you."

"I will." Stretching up, she kissed his cheek.

"Are you ready?" Gabe walked out with his horse and Isabella's.

"I am." She looked back at Travis. "I'll see you in the morning."

Helping her into the saddle, he stepped back,
a lump forming in his throat when she rode away.

Chapter Eleven

Fort Connall, Montana

Shoving open the door to his office, Colonel Miles McArthur removed his gloves, slapping them against his thigh, a string of curses flowing from his mouth. Well over six feet tall with a wiry build and thick, dark hair, Miles could intimidate almost anyone by walking into a room. It wasn't his stature alone that gave men pause. His chiseled features and implacable tone stalled many conversations before they started.

"Did you find any sign of the deserters, Captain?"

"No, sir. Like the last time, Sergeant Dowling had his men split up, taking different routes away from the camp they set up along Wildfire Creek." Captain Jonah Ryerson's mouth twisted into a grimace.

Miles snorted. "I won't have you referring to Dowling by rank, Captain. The man's a coward and a deserter. He'll face hanging once we capture and try him. I don't know how he managed to talk three privates and our Crow scout to join him."

"Plus two civilians, sir. A cook and one of the stable hands."

"He never should've been allowed to wear a uniform." Miles set down his hat, lowering himself into a chair. Scrubbing a hand down his face, he motioned for Jonah to sit down. "I fought with him at the end of the war. I've never encountered a man more brutal or soulless."

"I always thought since you were in the same cavalry division with him during the war, you asked for him to be assigned here."

Miles barked out a mirthless laugh. "Hell no. I requested the transfer to Montana. Dowling was sent out here as punishment for stealing ordnance. He should've been court-martialed and sent to prison, but the Army needed men out west. It was my bad fortune they sent him here."

Opening a drawer, he stared down at the faded image of his wife. The woman he'd loved more than his own life. The same woman who'd run away with his best friend while Miles served his country.

As the only remaining token of their union, he knew he should burn it. Instead, he kept it as a reminder of his poor judgment, the reason he'd requested a transfer thousands of miles away from their hometown of Baltimore.

Slamming the drawer shut, he picked up a message, sending a piercing glare at Jonah.

"A messenger arrived with this while you were on patrol." He shoved it across the desk.

Jonah glanced at Miles before picking it up. He could tell by the colonel's expression whatever it contained wasn't good. Reading it, the news couldn't have been worse.

"One man dead and two injured, including a child." He shifted his gaze to Miles. "You think it's Dowling and his men?"

"His band of thugs, Captain. Did you see the reference to one of them appearing to be an Indian?"

Jonah blew out a breath. "Black Feather. I don't know how Dowling convinced him to leave. He's been the fort scout for years."

"Money. It's a powerful incentive for men who have none."

Jonah's mouth twisted. "They killed a man."

"And they'll kill more if they aren't found and captured."

"The sheriff who sent this..." Jonah looked at the message again, "Gabe Evans, is asking for our help to search for them. It's doubtful he knows they're our deserters."

Miles crossed his arms. "Hell, Captain. We don't know if the men who robbed the bank and killed the man are ours. We're staring at assumptions here, but assumptions are all we've got. They figure six or seven men, at least one with a Union hat and another who they believe is an Indian."

Jonah leaned forward, handing the message back to Miles. "Do you want me to prepare some men to ride to Splendor?"

"It's not our job."

"But, Colonel—"

Miles didn't wait for him to finish. "We double our search patrols. Protecting the town is the job of their sheriff and his deputies. Finding the deserters is ours. It's our only duty right now, Captain Ryerson. Am I clear?"

Standing, Jonah squared his shoulders and saluted. "Quite clear, sir."

Splendor

"What does the message say?" Mack Mackey, one of Gabe's deputies, stood next to the desk, his hands resting on the edge as he leaned forward.

Shaking his head, Gabe tossed the paper down. "Colonel McArthur says they have no men available to help our search."

"That's it?" Caleb Covington, another deputy, sat down, his mouth twisted in disgust.

Gabe nodded. "I'm afraid so. It appears it's up to us to track them."

"Or prepare for another attack." Dutch McFarlin, a former Pinkerton Agency detective, who turned in that badge for one representing Splendor, leaned his shoulder against a wall, crossing his arms.

"What do you mean?" Caleb asked.

"In my opinion, we have two choices. Patrol the town and watch for anything unusual or form a group to go after the robbers. Going after them will leave Splendor without full protection. According to Clausen, they didn't get away with much. I'm thinking the gang may come back for what they missed the first time."

Steepling his fingers under his chin, Gabe nodded. "I've spoken to Cash and Beau about this. They feel the same as you, Dutch."

Mack nodded. "Since they're our best trackers, I'd be inclined to go along with them."

"What about you, Caleb?"

"I agree, Gabe. The colonel isn't willing to help, and we don't have enough men to track the robbers and protect the town. All of us believe they'll come back. The best move is to prepare for when they return."

Gabe nodded. "Then it's agreed. Tomorrow is Sunday. I'll need all of you at the church, with your guns. When the service ends, Cash, Beau, and I will walk out first, check the trail. The rest of you will stay inside. Don't let anyone leave until you get word from me. Understood?"

"Yes, sir," Caleb said at the same time Mack and Dutch nodded. "That's not all we have to watch, Gabe."

"What do you mean?"

Crossing his arms, Caleb leaned back in his chair. "You know the group of Chinese who left the mine?"

Gabe lifted a brow. "I know they rented some storefronts from Noah and Abby."

In a strange twist, Gabe's adopted son, Jack, inherited the Devil Dancer Mine when his father, a man he never knew, was killed. Lena oversaw all the legal matters, while Gabe took on the job of helping hire and protect the miners.

"They're opening a laundry, a restaurant, and a shop selling herbs." Caleb grinned at the dubious look on Dutch's face. "For medicinal uses. Turns out one of the miners is Yee Fan-Chung, a doctor from China. He's been treating sick and injured workers at the Devil Dancer."

"I've met him." Gabe rubbed his chin. "I wonder how he and the others got enough money to leave the mine."

Caleb scratched his chin. "I thought you or Lena would know."

Gabe shook his head. "All I know is the ones leaving are older workers with other professions in China."

"It could be they sent for money from family back home," Dutch said.

Gabe shifted his gaze to Caleb. "What does all this have to do with you saying we have to keep watch?"

Lips twisting into a grim smile, Caleb nodded toward the window. "Seems there are some shop owners in Splendor who aren't too happy with the Chinese opening stores."

Mack raised a brow. "It isn't against the law."

Caleb shook his head. "No, it isn't. That doesn't stop them from talking about it, usually over a few whiskeys at the Dixie or Wild Rose."

Letting out a frustrated breath, Gabe stood, sending a steady look at Caleb. "What you're saying is not only do we have to keep watch for the outlaws, we also need to watch our own citizens so they don't go after the Chinese."

Standing, Caleb nodded. "That sums it up."

Walking to the window, Gabe glanced outside, seeing a quiet town on a Saturday afternoon. Turning back, he looked at his men.

"Our priority right now is to keep the townsfolk safe from the outlaws. I can't explain it, but my gut tells me they'll be back. Maybe not tomorrow, but soon. In the meantime, everyone is to be on guard. If you hear anyone threaten to hurt the Chinese, I want to know right away."

Ginny handed Cooper to Isabella, allowing Luke to help her from the carriage. She held the months old baby, rubbing his back in gentle circles while Ginny straightened her dress. Before she could hand Cooper back, Cash and Allie walked toward them, drawing them into a conversation.

Isabella didn't mind. She could spend hours with him and never grow tired. Lowering her head, she rubbed her cheek against his hair, inhaling the scent unique to babies. Shifting Cooper in her arms, she didn't notice Travis watching her from several yards away, an unreadable expression on his face.

"Are you planning to sit up there all day?"

Travis tore his gaze from Isabella, waiting for the familiar pain to rip through him. How many times had he seen his wife holding their daughter the same way, cooing in the baby's ear, smiling up at Travis as he stared down at them? This morning, sitting atop Banjo outside the church, he didn't feel the familiar ache of loss. Instead, a surge of longing wrapped around him, causing his breath to catch.

"Hey, Dixon. Did you hear me?"

Giving a quick shake of his head, Travis glanced at Dirk. "Yeah, I heard you." Sliding to the ground, he moved his gaze back to Isabella, a lump forming in his throat. "I'll see you inside, Dirk."

Walking to the buggy, he tossed Banjo's reins over the back, then held out his arms. "May I?"

Isabella whipped her head toward him, a smile lighting up her face. "If you're sure."

"I am." He took Cooper from her, balancing him in one arm while helping her down. "He's getting big."

Brushing hands down her skirt, she adjusted her hat before looking at him. "Yes, he is. Before long, he'll be trying to walk. Then the work will begin."

Travis chuckled, staring into Cooper's eyes. "Yeah. I remember." Again, he steeled himself for the flash of pain, surprised when it didn't come.

"I'm sure she was gorgeous."

Raising a brow, he looked at Isabella. "Who?"

She took a step closer. "Your daughter."

Nodding, he shoved aside the regret. "She was beautiful." He glanced back at Cooper, clearing his throat. "Inside and out."

"Good morning, Travis. May I speak with you a minute?"

"Sure, Gabe." He handed Cooper to Isabella. "Excuse me a minute." He started to turn away, then stopped. "Do not go inside without me."

Isabella kept her smile in check, not wanting him to see how much pleasure his comment gave her. Focusing on the baby, she watched as the men walked several paces away.

Travis shot a look over his shoulder at Isabella, not wanting to leave her alone for long. He had no idea if David Peeler attended church, but he didn't plan to take any chances.

"What did you want to speak to me about, Gabe?"

"I see you have your gun."

Chuckling, Travis nodded, touching the handle with his hand. "I do."

"Don't take it off. Most of the men are going into church with theirs. We aren't going to let what happened to Albert occur a second time. My deputies and I are passing the word around." Gabe let his gaze move across the people outside the church. "When the service is over, Cash, Beau, and I will go outside first, make sure it's safe. Stay with Isabella and the others until one of the deputies lets you know it's all right to leave."

"Sure, Gabe. Do you want me to do anything else?"

"Nothing except help protect the women and children if the gang does ride in. Dutch, Mack, and Caleb will be staying inside."

"Don't worry, Gabe. We'll make sure the women and children are near the front of the church, away from the windows. Just don't expect us not to help if the outlaws show up and start firing at you." Travis clasped him on the shoulder. "That would be too much to ask."

A grim smile appeared on Gabe's face. "Thanks. You'd best get inside with the others."

Nodding, Travis wasted no time returning to Isabella, placing a hand on the small of her back. "Are you ready?"

"I am." Walking past Ginny and Luke, she gave a quick nod, letting them know she'd take Cooper inside. "Is everything all right?"

Travis couldn't help moving his gaze around the crowd of people, looking for anything or anyone appearing out of place. He glanced down at her and Cooper, his features softening.

"Everything is fine."

"You seem a little, well...tense."

He kissed her temple, not caring who might be watching. "Just anxious to get inside." Taking one more look around, he guided her into the church, steeling himself for whatever might happen.

Chapter Twelve

"Please, Papa. May I go with Grandfather and Baron Klaussner?"

Gabe glanced at Lena, knowing what she'd say. "You've got school."

"So does Johann, and *his* father is letting him go."

"The decision for Johann is up to his father." Gabe nodded at Jack's full plate of food. "Eat your supper, son."

Walter clasped his grandson on the shoulder, looking down the table at his son. "We'll be gone three days, Gabriel. Surely that isn't too much school to miss."

"It's rough territory at the north end of Redemption's Edge, Father. Then you come upon Blackfoot territory. Neither you nor Ernst know the area. Or the dangers."

Lena worried her lower lip, concern evident on her face. "And we don't know where the men who robbed the bank are hiding. Just because they didn't ride in again this morning doesn't mean they've left the area. What if you encounter them, Walter?"

"We'll all be armed. Certainly men such as those wouldn't harm a hunting party. I believe they'd be more apt to return to Splendor."

Gabe leaned forward. "No one knows what those men are planning. They may have moved on. But what if they haven't?"

"Do you truly believe the outlaws are camped close to Pelletier land? If they are intent on robbing a bank, or even a stagecoach, they'd be miles away from towns and main trails. Too far for any raids to be carried out."

Travis sat next to Isabella, his hand covering hers under the table. He always enjoyed the conversations at Gabe's house on Sunday afternoons. They'd grown livelier since Walter arrived from New York. His short visit had extended into weeks, then months. No one seemed in a hurry for him to leave.

"I must say, the trip does sound like fun."

Lena's jaw dropped. "Isabella, you do know the hunt will be long days, meager food, and cold nights on the ground, right?"

Walter cleared his throat. "Not so, Lena. Ernst will be bringing his large wagon, plus another for supplies, and his cook."

Isabella's brows rose. "The one who works with the chef at the Eagle's Nest?"

"The same." Walter leaned back in his chair. "There will be tents, privacy, and wonderful food. Oh, and he's bringing Ulrich."

Gabe cocked his head. "Ulrich Bernard, the man who rode into town with him? I thought he went back to New York."

"Only to settle some business issues. He returned a few days ago."

Travis looked at Gabe. "Who's Ulrich Bernard?"

"What would you call him, Father?"

Scratching his chin, Walter's mouth curled into a slight grin. "I believe he's Ernst's steward. Ulrich hires the servants, keeps the accounts, and manages domestic concerns. He is also Ernst's closest friend. They grew up together. Ulrich's father was the steward for Ernst's father. The way I understand it, the title is passed on from generation to generation, much the same as for the nobility."

Isabella looked at Walter. "How many servants does the baron have?"

"Five, I believe. He brought them from New York knowing he'd be building a large home. Ernst didn't know what to expect, what kind of people he'd find so far west." Walter took a sip of coffee, then cradled the cup with his hands. "Don't repeat this to him, but I believe he sees them as a part of his family. From what I've seen, they respect Ernst a great deal."

"I'd like to go."

Everyone's gaze shifted to Isabella, Travis's face twisting in shock. "Go where?"

She touched his arm. "With the baron and Walter, of course."

"No." The word burst from Travis's mouth before he could stop it.

Cocking a brow, Isabella shot him a stern glare. "No?"

Travis held firm. "I mean, you aren't going on a hunting trip with a group of men."

"Johann is going, and he's twelve."

Jack's face brightened. "Can I go if Aunt Isabella goes?"

Lena shook her head. "Jack, please let the adults talk about this."

Slumping back in his chair, Jack's face crumbled.

Travis let out a frustrated breath. "Johann is the baron's son, Isabella. Why would you want to go on the trip? You've never mentioned a desire to hunt. Wasn't yesterday the first time you'd held a six-shooter?"

"Yes, and you said I was quite good."

Closing his eyes, Travis tilted his head to the ceiling.

"Isabella, hunting the way the baron and my father plan to do it may sound simple, but it's not. You'll be walking through thick scrub most of the day, standing for long periods, getting dirty, and carrying a rifle or shotgun." Gabe glanced at his father, then back at Isabella. "After a while, they become heavy and uncomfortable. By the end of the day, your feet will hurt, maybe your stomach, and quite possibly your head."

Walter nodded. "So true. This is not a soirée, Isabella."

She placed a hand over her mouth to stifle a laugh. "Of course it isn't."

Taking her hand in his, Travis rubbed his thumb over her palm. "It's not a place for a woman."

Her breath caught at the sensations running through her. Arnott had never done anything causing such a strong rush of heat to stream down her arms and legs. Pulling her hand away, she licked her lips, lifting her chin.

"I don't know why not. I'm a widow, after all. Hardly some maiden who requires a chaperone."

Travis glanced across the table, his eyes pleading. "Lena?"

Holding up her hands, she shook her head. "I'm sorry, Travis. Isabella is a grown woman, capable of making her own decisions. If Walter and Ernst agree to her going, there's nothing I can do...or would do."

Travis shifted his gaze to Walter. "You wouldn't seriously consider taking her, would you?"

"Well, I..." Walter glanced around the table, seeing Isabella's expectant gaze and the warning on Gabe's face. "It isn't my decision. Ernst invited me, suggesting Jack come along to keep Johann company."

"See, Mama. Baron Klaussner wants me to come."

Lena looked down at him, settling her hand on his shoulder. "We'll speak about this later, Jack."

"But, Mama..." His lower lip stuck out, prompting Isabella to look away before he saw the amusement on her face.

"I said later, Jack. Do I need to send you to your room?"

Letting out a deep sigh, he shook his head. "No."

Lena nodded. "Good."

"Do you think the baron would mind me coming along, Walter?"

Shifting in his seat, he sent a quick, apologetic look at Travis.

"Honestly, I think he would approve of you going, Isabella."

Clasping her hands together, a broad smile broke across her face. "Wonderful. When do we leave?"

Looking at the others, the smile remained in place until her gaze settled on Travis. His jaw locked, a muscle in his temple pulsing. She felt, as well as saw, the anger on his face. Reaching over, she placed a hand on his arm.

"It will only be for a few days, Travis. I'll be fine."

Allowing himself a moment to regain his composure, his steely gaze met hers.

"You're darn right you'll be fine. I'm coming with you."

Redemption's Edge

Travis stuffed ammunition into his saddlebags, cursing under his breath. The day before, he'd left Gabe's not long after supper, baffled by Isabella's refusal to forget about joining the hunting party. Her interest made no sense to him, and no matter how she explained her reasons, he had to accept his woman was more stubborn than he'd imagined.

His hand stilled in the process of loading more items into the bag. *My woman.*

The thought had him lowering his head, shaking it to clear the image of a beautiful woman with dark hair and an easy smile. Placing a shaky hand against his chest, he pushed, trying to relieve the pressure created whenever he thought about Isabella.

This time, however, he forced himself to consider why he continued to deny his feelings. Shuddering at the image of two gravesites, he accepted he had two good reasons for not expressing how he felt. After losing his wife and daughter, the thought of remarrying and having more children terrified him. The notion of losing Isabella sent an icy chill through him, unlike anything he'd felt since the deaths of his family. Travis would rather face a gang of murderous outlaws than allow a break in his thick wall of emotional detachment.

"Are you leaving this evening?" Wyatt stopped a few feet away, aware of the turmoil surrounding his friend.

Nodding, Travis turned to look at him. "Unless you need me to stay."

Wyatt shook his head. "We completed one of the contracts last week and have plenty of time to fulfill the next one. A hunting trip would be good for you."

Travis pinched the bridge of his nose. "How do you figure?"

Shrugging, Wyatt glanced behind him to see Dax approaching. "Maybe a few days with Isabella will help you decide what you want."

"Wyatt tells me you're going on a hunting trip." Dax glanced at the bulging saddlebags and extra canteen attached to Travis's saddle.

"Yes, sir. Unless you need me here."

Crossing his arms, Dax shook his head. "We're good for a few days. Besides, I think it will be good for you to get away for a bit."

Snorting, Travis shot a quick glance at Wyatt. "Why is that?"

Chuckling, Dax placed a hand on Travis's shoulder. "It's something you're going to have to figure out for yourself." Switching his gaze to Wyatt, Dax inclined his head toward the house. "Do you have a few minutes before you head home?"

"As much time as you need." Wyatt glanced at Travis. "Wait up and I'll ride to town with you."

Letting out a breath, Travis turned his attention to packing the last items, wondering what Dax meant. He closed the saddlebags, removing his hat to shove a hand through his hair. Turning the hat in his hands, he considered what both men had said, his mouth twisting into a rueful grin.

He'd thought the only reason for joining the hunt was to keep Isabella safe. His friends made it clear they thought otherwise. Perhaps they were right.

"I appreciate you letting me spend the night, Gabe." Travis sat next to Isabella at the supper table, stabbing a piece of meat and putting it into his mouth.

Gabe set down his glass. "Makes sense with you leaving at sunrise."

Walter sliced through the roast, looking at Travis. "Thank you for going through the supply wagon. I know Ernst felt better having you check over what we're taking."

Travis and Wyatt had arrived in town to see Ulrich Bernard working with another man to fill the supply wagon they'd be taking on the hunting trip. Stopping to introduce himself, he'd been roped into inspecting the contents of the wagon, making suggestions to add some items and leave others behind. It didn't take long, giving him a chance to speak with Ernst and Ulrich about their destination. He'd been surprised to learn a guide hadn't been hired, someone who knew the territory and the potential dangers.

"I believe Ernst is quite pleased to have someone who knows the area going with us."

The glass Travis held stopped partway to his mouth. "I know Redemption's Edge and the territory north of it, but I've never hunted it.

When we wanted venison, I'd ride south, below the original Frey ranch."

Gabe looked at his father. "That land is now owned by the Pelletiers."

Walter scratched his chin. "Should we change our plans and go in that direction?"

Shrugging, Travis took a moment to consider the idea. "I believe we'll have better luck going north. The terrain isn't as rugged up there." He glanced at Isabella, seeing her raise a brow. "It'll be easier for the wagons north of Redemption's Edge. The southern section is rockier, with narrow, twisting trails. That's why Dax and Luke didn't raise cattle down that way. It was better suited for training horses."

"Papa says I can take his shotgun, Mr. Dixon." Jack's eyes lit up, a broad smile breaking across his face.

Travis looked at Gabe, then back at the boy. "Is that so?"

"Yes, sir. He says you can help me with it. Right, Papa?"

"That's what I said, son. You've had enough practice with it, so you shouldn't have to bother Mr. Dixon too much."

Travis turned toward Gabe. "It's no problem. I'll be helping Isabella and possibly Johann."

"I'm certain Ernst will be grateful for any advice you can provide to Johann. I'd also appreciate your expertise, Travis." Walter finished the last bite on his plate, sliding it a couple inches away.

"Jack, if you're finished, please say goodnight. You'll be up early tomorrow."

Lower lip jutting out, he looked at Lena. "It's not that early, Mama."

"Jack?"

He turned his head to look at Gabe, his shoulders slumping. "Oh...all right, Papa." Sliding from his chair, he started to pick up his plate.

"I'll take care of it, Jack." Isabella pushed away from the table, stopping when Lena stood.

"You finish getting ready for tomorrow, Isabella. Gabe will be happy to help me in the kitchen." Lena smiled at her husband, enjoying the resigned expression on his face.

Leaning toward her, Travis lowered his voice. "Do you have much more to pack?"

"Not really. You told me to take only what I needed."

"Did you include a pair of pants and boots?"

Her mouth tipped up into a wry smile, her voice sweet as honey. "Yes, I did. I packed what you told me to, Travis."

Chuckling, he stood, pulling out her chair. "If no one minds, Isabella and I are going to take a walk before turning in." He held out his hand.

Her eyes widened as she threaded her fingers through his. "We are?"

"Yes, we are." He ignored the hint of amusement on Gabe's face. Letting go of Isabella's hand, he placed his on the small of her back as they headed outside.

She looked around, her eyes crinkling at the corners. "It's a beautiful night."

He didn't respond as he guided her down the steps to a path leading around the house to the creek in back. "I thought we could spend a few minutes alone. After tonight, we'll have little privacy." Settling an arm around her waist, he led them down the path. "Have you heard any more from Mr. Peeler?"

Groaning, she looked up at him. "No, and I hope I don't."

"You know he won't give up."

Letting out a breath, she leaned into him. "I know. It's so hard to believe Arnott would discuss the matter with David and not me. You would've had to know him, but he and I discussed everything. He never would've left me out of something so important."

Travis stopped, turning her to face him. "So you don't believe David's story?"

Gazing into his eyes, she shook her head. "No, I don't."

"Good." Leaning down, he crushed her to him, his mouth covering hers in a hungry kiss. Feeling her cling to him, he deepened the kiss, hearing a ragged sigh escape her lips. Gentling his hold, he pulled back, taking in the glazed look in her eyes. "We're too close to the house to do what I want."

Raising a hand, she touched his face. "And what would that be, Mr. Dixon?"

"Ah, Isabella," he whispered, brushing a strand of hair from her face. "I'm certain you know what I want to do."

"And I'm as certain that I want you to do it." She watched his mouth open, then close, his eyes burning with something she couldn't quite define. "We're adults who've been married before. There's nothing stopping us from, well...from..." She wanted to say *making love*, but the words stuck in her throat. "From being together."

He brushed a kiss across her lips, then stepped away. "It isn't that simple."

"Why not?"

Scrubbing a hand down his face, he looked at her. "Because it isn't."

Crossing her arms, she cocked her head. "Do you find me so unattractive?"

His eyes bulged, jaw tightening. "Now that's a fool thing to say, Isabella. You're the most beautiful woman I've ever known."

"Then what is it?"

Pacing away a few feet, he fisted his hands on his hips, staring at the ground. A few moments went by before he turned to lock his gaze with hers. "I want you so much I ache with it, Isabella. You're the only woman I've wanted since my wife died, the only person who understands what I've gone through."

Walking up to him, she placed a hand on his arm, her voice softening. "That makes no sense. You want me and I want you. Why are you so hesitant?"

Closing his eyes, Travis grit his teeth. Opening them, he gripped her shoulders, staring into her upturned face. "It's not the time, Isabella." Dropping his hands, he moved farther away, shifting his gaze from hers.

"You still love your wife." Her whispered words held no censure, only a painful understanding.

"No...yes. Ah, hell..." He shook his head, not knowing how to express his feelings.

"It's all right, Travis. I will always love Arnott, although I'm certain it's not in the same way you loved your wife."

His gaze shot to hers. "What do you mean?"

Letting out a deep sigh, she walked past him, then stopped. "Your love was built on passion and desire. My marriage survived on mutual respect and friendship." She turned, taking a couple more steps before glancing over her shoulder. "Perhaps you're right. I've no idea how to fill the void she left in your heart." A sad smile tipped up the corners of her mouth before she turned back toward the house.

"Isabella, wait."

Halting, she shifted enough to look at him. "It's all right, Travis. There's no need to speak of it anymore tonight."

She hurried inside. Under no circumstances would she let him see the tears forming in her eyes. She didn't know if he meant to reject her, or if there were other reasons for his caution. Still, her heart cracked with a searing pain that felt the same as being discarded.

Chapter Thirteen

Travis forced his gaze away from Isabella and the enticing image of her wearing pants. They fit as if they'd been made specifically to hug her waist and hips, creating a distraction he didn't need. And he certainly didn't want any of the other men to see her this way. His options were slim. Travis had been the one to suggest she leave her dresses behind.

Helping Ulrich rearrange bags in the supply wagon, he peered at the others preparing to leave. Even Johann, with his furtive glances, couldn't hide his fascination with the way she looked. Travis doubted the twelve-year-old had ever seen a woman in pants. Judging by their expressions, perhaps the same could be said of Walter, Ernst, and Ulrich.

Travis shifted toward the eastern mountains, the sun glowing with the first rays of morning. If he hurried, he might have time to ride back to Gabe's and grab a couple dresses.

"Baron. We are ready to leave."

Cringing at Ulrich's announcement, Travis mumbled a curse, chastising himself for being the one who'd convinced her pants would be more appropriate than a skirt. He'd been a fool to suggest it.

"Quite so, Ulrich." Ernst walked toward Travis. "Are you satisfied with our provisions, Mr. Dixon?"

Chuckling, he stared at the wagon. "You have enough supplies for two weeks and twice as many people, Baron."

"Very good. I've found it always best to be overprepared. Don't you agree?"

It's your money, Travis thought. "I've no objection to your thinking."

"Excellent. Then we shall be off when everyone is ready."

Unable to put it off any longer, Travis grabbed Banjo's reins, walking toward Isabella. He'd ridden into town ahead of her, wanting to check the wagons one more time. She'd arrived with Gabe, a coat covering a man's shirt and her new pants. It had taken no more than five minutes for her to shed the coat to help Jack and Johann with their belongings.

Touching the brim of his hat, he focused on her face. "Good morning, Isabella." His chest squeezed at her brilliant smile.

"Good morning, Travis. It's going to be an extraordinary day, isn't it?" Nothing in her voice or stance indicated she held any anger toward him for the way they'd parted the previous night.

Shielding his eyes from the glare of the early morning sun, he nodded. "I suppose." Dropping his hand, Travis studied her face, deciding the slim-brimmed hat wouldn't work in the intense sun.

"You need a better hat."

Lifting her hands, she adjusted it to shield more of her face. "Is that better?"

"Better, but not good enough."

Scrunching her face, she tried again. "How is that?"

Shaking his head, he tried to not show how her efforts amused him. "You'll need a *different* hat."

Face falling, she removed the hat, staring down at it. "This is the only one I brought."

"I have another hat in my room." Johann moved closer, his face bright with excitement. "Shall I get it, Mrs. Boucher?"

She touched his shoulder. "That would be wonderful. Hurry, though, so we don't hold up the others."

Travis grabbed Johann's arm before he could rush past. "Do you have another pair of gloves?"

"Yes, sir."

"Bring them, too."

Nodding, Johann ran into the St. James, Jack not five paces behind him.

A faint blush crept up her face as she watched the boys disappear inside the hotel. "Thank you. I didn't think about a better hat."

Travis looked down at her hands. "And your gloves?"

A self-deprecating grin twisted her mouth. "They're still on my bed. I was so excited and in such a hurry, well..." She shrugged, noticing the glint in his eyes. "Do you find this amusing, Mr. Dixon?"

"No, Mrs. Boucher. I find you charming." He didn't have a chance to hear her reply before Ernst shouted for them to mount up. "You'll be riding next to me in the back. Jack and Johann will be in the middle, with Walter and Ernst in front."

Catching her lower lip between her teeth, she tilted her head, her gaze landing on the two older men. "Is that wise? For them to be in front, I mean. Neither one of them knows the territory."

Travis shook his head. "It's not wise, but it's what the baron wants. He's paying for this hunting trip, so that makes him the boss."

"I have what Mrs. Boucher needs." Johann handed her the hat and gloves.

"Thank you, Johann." Settling the hat on her head, she looked at Travis. "Is this better?"

Reaching up, he adjusted it slightly. "Much."

Isabella lifted her face, eyes widening. "Oh no."

Travis crossed his arms, an amused expression on his face. "What now?"

"Look." She nodded past him.

Turning, his smile faded. "What the hell is he doing here?"

David Peeler rode toward them, bouncing in the saddle, appearing more than a little uncomfortable atop the large roan. "Good morning, Isabella."

"David. What are you doing here?"

A nervous frown appeared, his gaze moving between Isabella and Travis. "Baron Klaussner invited me. I dined with him one night and he mentioned the hunt. I'm quite pleased to be included."

She had no time to respond before Walter came strolling toward them. "Good morning, David. I see you were able to join us."

"Yes, sir. I'm excited to see the wilderness I've heard so much about."

Travis lifted his head, staring into the early morning light, mumbling an oath.

"Is everyone prepared to leave?" Walter's gaze stopped on Jack.

"Yes, Grandfather. We're ready." Jack's voice squeaked with excitement.

"Excellent. Baron Klaussner says it's time to leave. Do you need any help, Jack?"

Shaking his head, Jack rushed to his horse. Holding the saddle horn, he jumped, his left foot catching in the stirrup before he swung into the saddle.

Walter chuckled at the speed Jack mounted his horse. "Appears the boy follows after his father. I'll let Ernst know we're ready. David, you'll be riding in front."

"Is that where you'll be, Isabella?"

"No, David. I'll be with Travis in the back. Enjoy your morning." Grabbing Blossom's reins, Isabella followed Jack's lead, settling herself into the saddle, pointedly ignoring David's scowl before he kicked his horse and followed Walter.

Travis's initial surprise at seeing David wore off as he stood next to Banjo, watching Isabella get comfortable. She caught his stare and squirmed, noticing his gaze wander from her boots up her legs to where she sat in the saddle.

"Is something wrong?"

Giving his head a quick shake, Travis swung up onto his horse, forcing his thoughts from the beautiful woman a few feet away. Clearing his throat, he focused on Ernst and Walter, who were already on the move.

"Not at all, sweetheart," he mumbled to himself before glancing behind him. "Let's go."

Over an hour into the ride, Ernst signaled for the group to stop, his expression bleak. Dismounting, he took long strides past Jack and Johann, coming to a stop next to Travis.

"Do you know where we are, Mr. Dixon?"

"Yes, sir. We're still on Pelletier land. Another hour and we should be close to the northern edge of their property."

"Good. Since you know where we are, I believe you should take the lead, Mr. Dixon."

Leaning forward, Travis rested his arms on the saddle horn. "If that's what you want."

Turning in a slow circle, Ernst took in the miles of open land before him, mountains on the west, rolling hills to the east. Nothing from the last hunt looked familiar.

"Yes, it is. Isabella may ride with Walter, David, and I."

"She stays with me, Baron." Travis's voice indicated no room for negotiation.

A knowing grin crossed Ernst's face. "Of course, Mr. Dixon." Taking another quick look around, he turned to leave.

"Baron?"

"Yes?"

"I'd appreciate it if you'd call me Travis."

He gave a brisk nod. "And you shall call me Ernst." Turning on his heel, he hurried back to the front.

"What did he want?"

As always, the sound of Isabella's voice sent a burst of pleasure through him. Reining Banjo around to face her, he motioned toward the front.

"Ernst wants me to take the lead. You'll be going up front with me."

She nodded at Jack and Johann. "What about the boys?"

"They'll stay where they are, behind us and in front of Ernst and Walter. The wagons will continue at the back. Come on. You'll enjoy it up there."

Reining Blossom to follow him, Isabella gave David a curt nod before taking in the vast landscape and beauty of the Pelletier ranch. "I had no idea their land extended this far north."

"Dax and Luke say it's the largest spread in western Montana. Some say it's the biggest ranch in the territory. I tend to agree with that. It won't be long before we'll need to move the herd up this way for a couple months."

"Do you just leave them here?" Isabella shifted in the saddle, clucking so Blossom kept pace with Banjo.

"There are always a few ranch hands who stay with the herd. The men rotate, each group staying a few nights."

Isabella watched him with a good amount of appreciation. A competent rider on a beautiful horse. "Is this what you do when you aren't training horses?"

Reaching behind him, he grabbed the canteen, holding it out to her. She took a small sip, then handed it back, watching as he took a long, slow swallow. Replacing the cap, he set it back behind him.

"Sometimes. Luke would rather Wyatt and I take a few men and search for wild mustangs. With the number of contracts they're getting, we can always use more horses. We couldn't possibly breed them fast enough to fulfill the need."

"Do you think I could ride with you sometime?"

His head whipped toward her. "Did I hear you right?"

Lifting her chin, she nodded. "I want to ride with you when you go after wild horses."

A curse almost slid past his lips before he caught it, stifling a groan. "No."

She blinked at his terse response. "No? You aren't even going to consider letting me come?"

Watching for the trail west he wanted to take, he shook his head. "That's right. You aren't riding along. Not while I'm riding for Redemption's Edge."

"And why not?" Isabella shot back.

"How many reasons do you want to hear?"

"Every one of them."

He opened his mouth to answer, closing it when a spot of color raced through the thick brush ahead of them. "Stay here."

"Stay? Travis, wait! Where are you going?" She almost rode after him, then considered the look in his eyes when he rode off. Determined, focused, and tolerating no argument from anyone, least of all her.

"Where is he going?"

"I don't know, Walter. He took off without an explanation."

Ernst and David joined them, each one concentrating on the spot where he'd entered the brush. Continuing forward at a slow pace, they reined up twenty yards from where they last saw him.

"Where is Mr. Dixon, Aunt Isabella?" Jack's worried voice caught her attention.

"He wanted to check on something, sweetheart. Travis asked that we all stay here."

Asked, she thought, a bitter taste forming in her mouth. She wished he'd *asked* instead of exploding away at a fast clip, causing her chest to tighten.

"Look. There he is." Johann pointed ahead of them to a trail a little farther north than the one he'd taken.

Isabella's lungs expanded, allowing her to breathe. She hadn't realized how much tension wrapped around her until he rode out of the forest, tall and confident in the saddle. He reined up beside them, frustration evident in his expression.

"I'm certain I saw something in the brush."

"Perhaps an elk or deer?" Ernst suggested.

Travis shook his head. "No. What I saw wasn't an animal."

Ernst's brows furrowed. "Not an animal?"

Narrowing his gaze on the spot where he'd first seen the flash of color, he shook his head. "I'm certain it was a man or boy. I saw a blaze of bright red. By the time I entered the brush, then the trees beyond, I'd lost him."

"One of your famous Indians." Ernst smiled. "How wonderful. We might see our first Indian, Johann."

"Can we go after him, Father?"

Travis stabbed the boy with an intense glare. "No one is going after anyone, Johann." He looked at Jack. "Do you both understand what I'm saying?"

Jack lowered his head, nodding. "Yes, sir. We understand."

"Johann?"

"I understand, Mr. Dixon."

"Good." Travis looked at Ernst. "I planned to enter the forest right about where I spotted, well…whatever it was I saw. Instead, I want to ride a little farther north, stay out in the open."

"Whatever you think best, Travis." Walter reined his horse around. "You're in the lead." Ernst followed, but David remained behind.

"Perhaps you should ride with us near the back, Isabella. Up here, you only have Mr. Dixon to protect you." David shot a hostile look at Travis.

Biting the inside of her cheek before she said what she thought, Isabella forced a sweet smile. "Thank you for your concern, but I feel quite safe up here, David."

"If you're sure…"

Chin tilted upward, she nodded. "I am quite certain."

Irritation flashed across his face before David covered it with congenial expression. "As you wish." He cast a vile look at Travis before reining his horse around.

Grateful David didn't continue to argue, Travis looked at Isabella, a knot forming in his stomach at the worry on her face.

"Is everything all right?" She did her best to hide the tremor in her voice.

Forcing a smile he didn't feel, he reached out to touch her arm. "Everything is fine. We're just going to take a different trail. One not as secluded, where we can see a good distance ahead of us."

He refused to confess the real possibility of running into a Crow hunting party. Travis had little concern about the Blackfoot village several miles north. Their chief, Running Bear, the Pelletiers, and Bull Mason had formed a friendship over the years. He and his grandson, Swift Bear, had even shown up unexpectedly when Bull and Lydia returned to town after a trip to San Francisco.

The Crow were the real threat. One he didn't intend to confront with a group of novice hunters.

"I want you to stay close to me, Isabella. If anything does happen, do exactly as I say without hesitation. Can you do that?"

"But you said nothing's wrong."

Doing his best to let the worry he felt fade away, he nodded to the trail ahead. "You can never be too careful in this country, Isabella. I can't say for certain what's ahead of us. That's why it's important for you to stay close and do as I say." He swallowed the concern building in his chest. "Trust me."

Tightening her hands on the reins, she nodded. "I've always trusted you, Travis."

Chapter Fourteen

Settling fisted hands on his hips, Travis made a slow circle, studying their camp. The trail he'd taken narrowed until the wagons could barely pass. Thankfully, it opened into a clearing large enough for Ulrich and the cook to drive the wagons into, less than fifty yards from Wildfire Creek. It would make a good base for the hunt, allowing them access to several trails to the west and north.

"Mrs. Boucher, you will be sleeping in the wagon."

Travis turned his head at Ernst's commanding voice. The baron may not have gotten them to this point, but he didn't hide his intention of leading the group from here on.

Isabella cast a quick glance at Travis. "Thank you for the generous offer, Baron. My preference is to sleep outside, under the stars."

Stepping next to her, Ernst's face clouded. "Sleeping on the ground can be quite uncomfortable. Are you certain you wouldn't want the comfort of the wagon, my dear?"

Though it didn't seem to bother Isabella, Travis cringed at Ernst's use of the endearment. Instead of staying within hearing distance, he took the trail toward Wildfire Creek, still concerned about what he'd seen earlier. He wasn't as good a tracker as Cash or Beau. Still, he had some skills, and walking the trail might help him see tracks he'd missed riding Banjo. Before moving into the brush, he spotted Isabella take a step away from Ernst, frustration tinging her features before she forced an indulgent grin.

"Truly, I'm perfectly fine sleeping outside. Excuse me. I want to speak with Travis about the best spot to place my bedroll."

Ernst touched a finger to his forehead in salute. "Of course. Please, let me know if you change your mind."

"I will," she tossed over her shoulder on her way to find Travis. Stopping in the center of the camp, her brows furrowed when she didn't see him.

"If you're looking for Mr. Dixon, he walked that way, Aunt Isabella."

She followed where Jack pointed. "Thank you. Will you be all right while I'm gone?"

He cocked his head, his mouth twisting into a grimace. "I'm not a baby any longer, Aunt Isabella."

Holding in a smile, she touched his shoulder. "Of course you aren't, Jack. You're quite the young man."

He seemed to grow taller at her compliment. "Mama told me the same."

"And she's right. Well, I'm going to speak with Mr. Dixon. I shouldn't be gone long."

"Would you like me to accompany you?"

This time, she bit her lower lip. Jack had grown up before her eyes and she'd almost missed it. "Thank you, Jack, but I'll be fine. I'm certain you and Johann have things you'd like to do."

His gaze shifted to where Johann stood with his father. "Well, we do have some ideas."

Chuckling, she touched his shoulder. "Then go along. I'll be fine on the trail by myself."

"Isabella, wait!" David rushed toward her.

She closed her eyes, grimacing at the shout from the other side of the camp. Releasing a sigh, she stopped. "What is it, David?"

"I thought we could take a walk, discuss what I mentioned the other day." When she didn't respond, he continued. "About Arnott's wishes."

"I know what you meant. I'd rather wait until we return to Splendor to talk about the letter."

Jerking his head around, making certain they were alone, he stepped closer. "Now is the perfect time, Isabella. We're alone, with no one to hear us."

Exasperation flashed across her face before she stilled her features. "I know you came a long way to deliver the message, and I do understand your concern about trying to fulfill what you believe to be my late husband's wishes. I hope you'll respect my desire to wait a little longer. I'm simply not prepared to comment on the note you brought. I need more time."

His lips drew into a thin line. "How much more time?"

"When do you plan to return to Philadelphia?"

He startled at her question. "I believe you mean when do *we* plan to return. The answer is, no date has been set."

She certainly didn't mean *we*, deciding not to address his assumption now. "Then it doesn't matter if the discussion is put off a few more days. Now, if you'll excuse me, I really must find Travis."

A deep scowl marred his face. "Tell me you aren't serious about such a rough man."

A slight blush tinted her cheeks, eyes boring into his. "I can assure you, I am quite serious about him, David."

He moved closer, his voice rising. "You can't possibly mean that. He's much too unsettled and dangerous for a sheltered woman such as yourself. Arnott would be quite displeased if he knew what you planned."

Anger rose, building in her stomach, then moving to her chest. "Do not tell me how Arnott would feel about my life. He's gone. I'm not. And I'll not have you, or anyone else, dictating what I should and shouldn't be doing. In case you haven't noticed, I'm a grown woman, perfectly capable of deciding my fate. I'll see you later, David." Shifting, she stalked down the trail, ignoring David's plea to stop, doing her best to push her fury aside.

The farther from camp she got, the better she felt, anger fading to delight as she spotted the creek ahead of her. She remembered the house Luke built along Wildfire Creek after returning from his last assignment as a Pinkerton agent. Bull designed it for him, while the ranch hands helped build the home he lived in when Ginny came into his life.

Isabella recalled it being peaceful, less than half a mile separating it from the main ranch house where Dax and Rachel lived. She hadn't been back to the creek since, had no idea how beautiful it could be surrounded by berry bushes and lush vegetation.

"What are you thinking?"

She whipped around, Travis's voice jolting her from her thoughts. "I didn't hear you approach."

He continued forward, stopping a few inches away. "That was the idea." Placing his hands on her waist, he drew her to him. "I was enjoying watching you." Leaning down, he covered her mouth with his. Moments passed as they pressed into each other, Isabella wrapping her arms around his neck, drawing him down.

Feeling his hands move to her back, she dug into his shoulders, a soft groan leaving her lips. Tracing the outline of his lips with her tongue, she sighed when he took control, angling his head, finding the access he sought.

"You've too many clothes on," he mumbled against her mouth, feeling her smile.

"You can change that." She chuckled as her hands moved to his chest, meaning to open his shirt.

"Aunt Isabella! Are you down here?"

Travis murmured a vague oath, setting her aside at Jack's voice.

"Aunt Isabella?"

She looked up at Travis, seeing the same regret on his face she felt. "We're by the creek, Jack."

A few seconds later, footfalls sounded on the trail before Jack and Johann burst through the bushes. "We've been looking for you." Jack's body surged with excitement.

"Is something wrong?" Travis asked.

Johann shook his head. "Father and Mr. Evans want to hunt this evening. Ulrich is preparing everything, but they want to speak with you first."

Rubbing the back of his neck, Travis shot a look of disappointment at Isabella. "Guess we'd better get back."

Jack jumped up and down. "You won't talk them out of it, will you, Mr. Dixon?"

Settling a hand on his shoulder, Travis turned him toward the trail. "Let's go find out what they have planned."

"Johann already told you. They want to hunt."

Scrubbing a hand down his face, Travis glanced at Isabella. A thin smile and shrug were her only answers.

"You're right, Jack. But if they want to hunt, they need to know what they're after, where they're going, and how long they'll be gone."

Johann spoke first. "I believe that is why they want to speak with you, Mr. Dixon. They aren't sure where to go or what to take."

They stepped from the shadowed, dense cover of the forest into the sun-filled clearing. Travis noted Ernst cleaning his rifle while Walter loaded ammunition into saddlebags. Hearing the snap of twigs, he looked up.

"Travis." Walter waved, motioning him forward.

"Johann and Jack told me you want to hunt this afternoon."

Ernst joined them, leaning on his rifle. "We'd like you to come with us, Travis."

Shifting his stance, he raised his head to the afternoon sun and took off his hat, checking the wind.

"Wind's picking up and the sun is moving toward the mountaintops. You'd have better luck waiting until early morning when everyone is fresh and the animals are out for their morning meal."

Ernst lowered his voice, turning away from Johann, who stood several feet away. "I promised my son we could hunt today."

"I can appreciate that, Ernst." Travis noticed the cook scurrying about, already preparing their evening meal. "We're only a couple hours from supper. My suggestion is we spend some time checking trails, see if we can spot any recent tracks, droppings...signs deer or elk have been here recently."

"Do you suggest we take our rifles?" Walter asked.

"Absolutely. I'm just saying don't get your hopes up. And you can remove about a fourth of the ammunition you've packed, Walter. We won't need a horse. If someone does get a deer or elk, I'll come back for one. When it starts to get dark, we head back to camp." Travis pierced Jack and

Johann with a stern gaze. "Do you boys understand me?"

"Yes, sir," they responded in unison before running back to get their rifles.

Travis turned to Ernst. "I hope I didn't overstep my bounds with Johann."

"Not at all. You know much more about hunting in these mountains than I do. Johann respects you, as do the rest of us." He looked to the sky. "We should leave soon."

Travis nodded. "Everyone should be ready in ten minutes."

His gaze moved past the happy faces of the two boys, who talked next to one of the wagons, searching for Isabella. Irritation rolled through him at the sight of her in what appeared to be an intense conversation with David. Arms crossed, she shook her head at something he said. Having seen enough, he strode toward them, putting a protective arm over her shoulders.

"Is something wrong, sweetheart?"

"This is a private conversation, Mr. Dixon." David's terse response had no effect on Travis.

"Would you like me to stay or leave, Isabella?"

She leaned into him, her voice clear and firm. "Stay. Whatever David has to say may be said in front of you."

"It seems the lady wants me to stay, Mr. Peeler. Please, go ahead with whatever you have to say."

Fisting his hands, David's features contracted, his mouth twisting into a sneer. "She's too fragile to be carrying a rifle and participating in a hunt. I asked her to stay in camp with me—"

"Which I refused to do, David."

"Regardless, this is not a sport for a lady, Isabella. Surely you know how Arnott would feel about you being out with a group of men, hunting wild animals."

Travis felt her body tremble. Believing it came from rage and not fear, he leaned forward, stopping her from verbally assaulting the man.

"Isabella will be with me. I assure you, she knows how to handle a rifle, a shotgun, and a revolver. If she didn't, I'd be the one telling her to stay behind."

"Because she can handle weapons doesn't mean she should go."

Hearing enough, she pushed away from Travis. "David, let me tell you what I am going to do. First, I'm accompanying Travis on today's hunt, as well as any others during our trip. Second—and this is important, so pay attention— I am not a frail female who needs you or any man to protect me. I choose to go with Travis because

I respect his judgment and skill. And third, I am quite proficient with a rifle."

Snorting, David let his gaze wander over her. "You're not much bigger than Johann, and I'm certain he has more skill than you."

Travis murmured an oath, tightening his grip on Isabella, sensing what was coming.

Twisting out of his grasp, she stepped to within a foot of David, pinning him with an angry glare. "If you're able to keep up with us, you might very well see how good I am with a rifle." She poked him in the chest. "You've become a pompous, miserable—"

Travis grabbed her around the waist, hauling her to him.

"What are you doing?" Isabella sputtered, her anger now directed at him.

Leaning down, Travis whispered in her ear. "Saving you from creating a spectacle in front of the others." He nodded to the center of the camp.

She followed his gaze, seeing Ernst, Walter, Ulrich, and the boys watching them. Swallowing her embarrassment, Isabella nodded. "You're right."

Feeling the fight leave her, he loosened his hold. "Is it safe to let you go?"

She looked up at him, amusement in her face. "Yes. I'm fine. Just keep him away from me." The last was said loud enough for David to hear.

Straightening her shoulders, she sucked in a ragged breath. "If you gentlemen will excuse me, I must get ready to leave with everyone else."

Travis waited until she'd put a good distance between them, then turned to David. "I'd suggest you give Isabella a little room, Mr. Peeler. I don't know what she was like in Philadelphia, but I can tell you, she's stronger than you seem to believe."

"Don't even consider lecturing me on Isabella. I've known her for years," he sniffed. "You've known her a scant few months, Mr. Dixon."

Lifting a brow, Travis shrugged. "Suit yourself. I'm just trying to keep you from getting shot while you're on this trip."

Crossing his arms, David jutted out his chin. "And just who do think would shoot me?"

Chuckling, Travis shook his head. "If you aren't careful...Isabella."

Chapter Fifteen

Yanking the blanket under her chin, Isabella drew her knees up to escape the cold chill. Sighing, she did her best to stay in the drowsy haze instead of opening her eyes. Rolling to her back, she grimaced, wondering at the sharp pain piercing her side.

Eyes popping open, her brain registered the darkness an instant before remembering she wasn't in her own bed. The immediate panic turned to awe as her eyes adjusted, seeing a thick blanket of stars. Staring at a full moon, a strange, yet comforting quiet wrapped around her.

"Beautiful, isn't it?"

Shifting, Isabella found herself staring into deep blue eyes mere inches from her face. Her initial confusion transformed into a sleepy smile, heart tripping at the gleam in Travis's eyes.

"Yes, it's quite beautiful."

"I never tire of waking to this when I'm out with the herd. Soon, you'll hear the sounds of morning as the birds and animals wake up."

The words barely left his mouth when a loud screech cut through the quiet. Startled, Isabella gasped, her eyes widening.

"Relax, sweetheart. It's just a hoot owl. They're real common in these parts. We've got several of them nesting around the ranch." He pulled an arm out from under his covers, reaching over to place it on her shoulder. "You'll get used to it."

She cringed as another screeching sound pierced the silence, then shuddered when a large form flew several feet above them.

She dragged the blanket over her head, peeking out at Travis. "What was that?"

His mouth turned up. "Probably the same hoot owl deciding it's time to look for food." When she started to lower the blanket, his gaze became serious. "I guess it could've been a bat."

"A bat?" Her voice wobbled, nose wrinkling.

"Big, brown, ugly things. They don't eat much, though." His lips twitched, watching the information roll around in her head. Seeing the amusement on his face, she lowered the blanket.

"You're teasing me."

A mischievous smile broke across his face. "Yep." Pushing out of the bedroll, he stood, stretching his hands above his head as he scanned the camp.

Sitting up, Isabella rubbed the sleep from her eyes. "Is anyone else awake?"

"Only the cook and Ulrich, but Jack and Johann are starting to stir."

She watched him stroll off into the bushes, then scrambled from the bedroll, grabbing her coat. Leaving her pants and shirt on had been a wonderful idea. Travis had talked her out of slipping into her nightgown, telling her how common it was to be woken by the sound of a nearby critter. The warning had her placing the rifle less than a foot away.

"Your turn."

She jumped and spun around. "How can you walk over all this dead brush and not make a sound?"

Looking behind him at the path he'd taken, Travis shrugged. "Practice?"

"Aunt Isabella! Are you ready to go?" Jack ran up, enthusiasm pulsing through him.

Hearing Travis chuckle, she looked at the young boy, wishing she had his energy. "I don't believe your grandfather or Baron Klaussner are up yet, Jack. Plus, you must have breakfast before starting out on a hunt. Isn't that right, Mr. Dixon?"

"But I'm not hungry," Jack protested, looking at Johann a few feet away, who nodded in agreement.

"Your aunt's right, Jack. Cook is already preparing breakfast, and Ulrich is organizing the gear. Maybe you two could go roust the others."

Sticking his lower lip out, Jack grimaced. "Do we have to take Mr. Peeler?"

Biting her lower lip, Isabella did her best to keep a straight face. "Don't you like Mr. Peeler?"

Jack and Johann shook their heads.

Letting out a weary breath, she settled a hand on Jack's shoulder. "He's the guest of Johann's father. We can't very well leave him behind, can we, Jack?"

Slowly shaking his head, the boy's mouth twisted. "No, I suppose not."

Giving them her best stern look, she nodded toward where the men were bunked down. "All right then. You two better hurry up and wake them."

Watching them run off, she turned toward Travis, shaking her head. "I certainly hope we see a deer or elk today."

Slipping into his coat, he rolled up his sleeping gear, holding it under his arm. "The tracks we found yesterday indicate the animals are around here. With any luck, we'll spot more than one."

"It's going to be hard keeping the boys quiet."

Travis glanced across the camp to where Jack and Johann were waking the men. "Not if we threaten them with the worst punishment."

Crossing her arms, she met his gaze. "And what would that be?"

"Sending them back to camp."

More than once, Travis thought he'd have to make good on his promise to return them to camp. After repeated warnings, neither seemed to comprehend the importance of staying out of sight and keeping quiet. Then Ernst spotted a deer on the other side of Wildfire Creek.

Seeing the animal grazing did more than words to silence them. Neither moved, not even to shoulder their rifles. They were so spellbound, both jumped when Ernst fired a shot, downing the unsuspecting buck.

Travis smiled. "Nice shot, Ernst. Let's go see how you did."

Crossing the creek, the group studied the buck before Travis and Ulrich hung it from a sturdy branch. Pulling out his knife, Travis began the process of preparing the animal for transport back to camp. The others stood around, Isabella with a hand over her mouth, eyes closed, while the boys did their best not to lose their breakfast.

David wasn't so fortunate. Five minutes into the process, he turned, dashing several feet away to retch against a tall pine.

Travis stilled at the sound, a small degree of pleasure seizing him at the other man's discomfort. Casting a quick glance at Ulrich, he was surprised to see the man's eyes gleam in understanding. Focusing again on the task before him, Travis finished quickly, motioning for Johann to bring the horse forward.

He'd just set the animal on the horse's back when a volley of gunfire sounded close by. Ignoring the deer as it slid to the ground, he drew his gun. Kneeling, Travis pulled Isabella down next to him, motioning for the others to find cover.

"Everyone get down."

Squirming, her frantic eyes searched for the boys. "I have to find Jack and Johann."

Tightening his hold around her waist, Travis shook his head. "Ernst and Walter have them." He nodded toward the other side of the creek, feeling her let out a strained breath, then shudder at the sound of more gunfire. "We have to move. Stay with me, Isabella."

Travis grabbed her hand, rushing behind a copse of thick bushes. Lifting his head, he looked around, hearing shouts and the sound of men trampling through the brush somewhere upstream. Leveling his gun in the direction of the noise, he waited, hoping Ernst and Walter were doing the same.

Minutes passed without more gunfire. Travis began to think whoever fired the shots had left when someone crashed through the bushes above them, racing toward the creek. Travis stilled, recognizing the young Indian.

Swift Bear's frantic gaze passed right over their hiding place, legs pumping, his face glistening with sweat. He'd almost made it to the water when another shot rang out, catching him in his shoulder. Stumbling, he tried to right himself without success before landing, face down, a few feet away.

"I got him!"

The shout turned Travis's concern into a mountain of rage. Rising, he aimed toward the sound of approaching voices. Before he could get off a shot, rifle fire flashed past him, stopping the advancing group. Seeing one raise his gun, Travis fired, hitting him in the chest. Ernst, Walter, and Ulrich continued to fire as two of the men chasing Swift Bear grabbed their wounded companion, then scattered into the forest.

Travis held up his hand, stopping Ernst, Walter, and Ulrich from pursuing them. They had a wounded boy to tend, and certainly didn't need anyone else getting shot.

After a full minute, Travis felt the danger had passed enough to scoot forward, staring at the boy's prone form. He could see where the bullet entered his left shoulder from behind. Turning him over, Travis let out a relieved breath, spotting the exit wound.

Shifting, he waved for the others. "Bring the horse." Shirking out of his coat, he unbuttoned his shirt, using it to stop the bleeding.

"I know him."

He glanced up at Isabella's whisper. She knelt next to him, holding the shirt in place on Swift Bear's chest while Travis pulled enough of the fabric around to cover the entry hole.

"Isn't this the boy who came to see Bull and Lydia when they returned from San Francisco?"

Travis nodded, motioning for Walter to hand him the canteen. "Yes. This is Swift Bear, Running Bear's grandson. I wonder what he's doing out here alone."

"What can I do?" Walter hovered above them, staring at the first Indian he'd ever seen.

"Any whiskey in the saddlebag?"

A grim smile curved Walter's mouth. Reaching into his coat, he pulled out a flask, handing it to Travis. Taking off the cap, he lifted his shirt, pouring the liquid over the wound on both sides. The boy didn't budge at the alcohol's burn.

"Get anything we can use to bind up his wound. I need to get him to the ranch."

Isabella gripped his arm. "I'm going with you."

Lifting his gaze, he nodded. "I wouldn't think of leaving you behind." With gunmen nearby, the entire group would pack up and return to open land, heading south to Redemption's Edge.

"Will this work?" Walter held out another shirt. "It's all I could find."

Isabella took the makeshift bandage, recognizing it as the shirt he'd worn when they started. "This will do fine, Walter. Thank you."

Between them, they had Swift Bear's wound dressed within minutes. Standing, Travis bent down, lifting the boy into his arms. Handing him to Walter, he mounted the horse, taking the Indian back into his arms.

"We have to get back to camp and let the cook know to pack up."

Understanding filled Walter's face as he watched the young man. "Do you know him?"

"He's Swift Bear. The Blackfoot chief's grandson."

"I'll tell the others. You ride on out. We'll do our best to keep up." Walter dashed across the creek, huddling with Ernst and Ulrich.

"You go ahead, Travis. I'll be with the others."

"I don't like—"

She held up her hand, cutting him off. "You have no choice. It isn't far. We'll be right behind you."

Pulling his gun from the holster, he handed it to her. "Shoot anyone you don't recognize."

"But I have my rifle."

"You may not have time to get a shot off. The six-shooter is fast. Don't hesitate. If anyone approaches, shoot first. Aim for the chest. Can you do that?"

Isabella stared at the gun. Lifting her face, she nodded.

Leaning down, he placed a quick kiss on her lips. "I'll start back as soon as I get Swift Bear into one of the wagons. Keep the boys close, stay low…and hurry."

Isabella's heart pounded as they made their way back to camp. Ernst took the lead while Walter and Ulrich stayed at the rear, glancing around and behind them as they made their way along the trail.

Everyone except David kept their rifles ready, a blanket of apprehension driving their pace. His color hadn't returned. He'd stopped twice, his skin sallow and pasty. The last time, Walter took him by the arm, forcing David to keep up, promising to leave him behind if he didn't.

Ernst stopped at a fork in the trail, looking around. "I believe camp is this way."

"No, Father. It's that direction." Johann pointed to the opposite trail.

Glancing around, Ernst looked at Walter. "What do you think?"

Shaking his head, he narrowed his gaze, trying to remember the correct path.

Isabella stepped between them. "I'm certain Johann is right."

No sooner had she spoken than Travis rode toward them from the direction Johann pointed. She sagged, relief rushing through her.

"Is everyone all right?"

"We're all fine, Travis," she breathed out, placing a hand on his leg.

Sliding to the ground, he took the rifle from her hand, setting it beside him before lifting her into the saddle.

"Travis, I can walk back."

He handed the rifle back to her, then glanced around. "Anyone have an objection to Isabella riding?"

No one objected, although the look on David's face said something different. Ignoring him, Travis lifted his gaze to meet Isabella's. Handing him back his gun, her mouth twisted into a worried frown.

"Don't stop and stay low in the saddle." He slapped the horse's rump. "We'll be right behind you, sweetheart." He looked at the others. "We must move fast."

Travis didn't wait for responses before taking the lead, a rifle in one hand, his revolver in the other. Swift Bear hadn't awakened before he left camp. The sooner they got going, the better the chance the young brave would make it to the ranch and into Rachel's care.

Redemption's Edge

"How long has he been like this?" Rachel directed Travis into a downstairs bedroom, pulling back the covers. Placing Swift Bear in the middle of the bed, he stepped back.

"Off and on for four, maybe five hours. Wakes for a minute or two, then nods off. He's got a gash on his head plus the gunshot wound. I did what I could, Rachel, but..." His voice trailed off as his worried gaze moved over Swift Bear.

Placing a hand on his arm, she looked at him. "You did fine, Travis. Now, let me get to work. Rosemary is at the clinic and Ginny is at their place. Please tell Isabella I'll need her help, plus warm water and clean rags. You'll find them in the closet off the kitchen next to a bottle of whiskey."

He rushed outside, bounding down the porch steps. "Rachel needs your help, Isabella. I'll bring the rest of what you'll need."

She dashed off as Dax rode up, reined to a stop, and dismounted. "What's going on?"

Placing fisted hands on his hips, Travis stared after Isabella. "We were hunting with Ernst and Walter. A group of men were chasing Swift Bear. One of their bullets caught him in the shoulder."

An oath flew out of Dax's mouth before he could stop it. "How is he?"

"Rachel's with him. The bullet went clean through, but he took a good hit to his head."

"Did you recognize any of them?"

"No. It happened fast. When Swift Bear fell, Ernst, Walter, Ulrich, and I started firing. The men scattered before I could get a good look. We shot at least one of them."

Dax shifted his stance, seeing Jack and Johann standing by one of the wagons. "How did the boys do?"

Travis followed his gaze, snorting. "Better than Isabella's friend, David Peeler."

"I don't believe I've met Mr. Peeler. You say he's her friend?" Dax lifted a brow.

"A friend of hers and her late husband. Says he traveled from Philadelphia to find her." His mouth twisted into a grimace. "He brought a letter Arnott supposedly wrote requesting David marry Isabella if he didn't pull through."

Dax threw back his head, laughing, then stopped at the sober expression on Travis's face. "You're not joking."

"Wish I were."

"What does Isabella think?" Dax glanced at the front door where she'd disappeared not more than a couple minutes before.

"I don't think she believes the letter is real. Although he was considerably older, they were very close and shared everything."

Dax nodded. "This doesn't sound like something he'd keep from her. When did this note materialize?"

"When Peeler arrived in town. He said Arnott wrote it the night before he died." Travis rubbed the back of his neck. "Isabella doesn't remember Peeler being at the house the night before her husband died, or for a few days before. Still, she's concerned Arnott did write the letter. If so, she might be driven by guilt to consider the marriage."

Crossing his arms, Dax studied him. "Are *you* concerned? If so, we can always find a way to make someone disappear."

Travis's surprised gaze shot to Dax, seeing the mirth on his face, his mouth curving into a smile.

"No?" Dax's eyes sparkled. "Then I guess we go the legal route and get some information on the man. I'll talk to Dutch McFarlin. That man's got the best sources of anyone I've ever met."

"Except for Allan Pinkerton."

"It's a good thing Dutch worked for the man. I can ask Luke to check around, too. Have Isabella put off Peeler as long as she can."

"From what I've seen, she won't be bullied into making a decision. Take whatever time you need." Travis grasped Dax's shoulder. "I appreciate anything you can do to clear this up." Turning to walk back into the house, he stopped at Dax's voice.

"When this is over with Peeler, you might consider asking that woman to marry you."

Grinning, he nodded. "You know, for once, Dax, you might have come up with a good idea."

Chapter Sixteen

Rachel soaked a cloth in cool water, wringing it out before placing it on Swift Bear's forehead. He'd woken twice, mumbling a few words before falling back into unconsciousness.

"Does he feel any cooler?" Isabella prepared another cool cloth, handing it to Rachel.

"Not really. I don't see any signs of infection, which is what worries me. Usually, a fever would be an indication the wound has putrefied." Rolling her shoulders to release the tension, she swapped the original cloth with the cooler one. "I need to send for my uncle or Doc McCord."

"Ernst and the others have already left for town. I'll find Travis and let him know."

"Tell him to hurry, Isabella. We need to get Swift Bear through this as fast as we can."

Her face etched with worry, Isabella hurried out of the room, finding Dax, Travis, and Wyatt in the study. "Rachel needs one of the doctors. Can someone ride into town?"

Wyatt stood. "I'll go. Does she want her uncle or Clay McCord?"

"It doesn't matter. Whoever comes, he needs to get here as soon as possible."

Seeing her shoulders slump with fatigue, Travis walked up to her, settling an arm over them. "Has he woken up?"

"A couple times, then he nodded off again. His temperature keeps rising and we can't get it down." She turned to Wyatt. "Please tell the doctor Rachel can't find any signs of infection."

"I will. I'll be back as soon as I can."

"Wait up, Wyatt, and I'll ride with you. I want to talk to Dutch about sending a telegram." Dax looked at Travis, seeing understanding in his eyes.

After Wyatt and Dax walked out, Travis turned Isabella toward the kitchen. "Let's get you and Rachel some coffee. I'm guessing neither of you have relaxed since we arrived with Swift Bear."

Entering the kitchen, Travis stepped in front of her, pulling her close. Letting her sag against him, he felt her tremble as soft sobs began to soak his shirt. Tightening his hold, Travis rested his chin on the top of her head, stroking her back. After a few moments, she lifted her head, eyes red-rimmed.

"I'm usually not so emotional."

"If anyone has a right to be emotional, it's you. I'll bet you've never been shot at before."

She shook her head.

"Or seen someone shot."

"No. Never."

"It would shake anyone up, Isabella."

"Not you."

He let out a breath, a remote memory igniting of the first time he saw a comrade fall in his first battle of the Civil War. "Believe me, the first time wasn't good. He was a friend, a man I respected. We were laughing about something a moment before the battle started. A few seconds later, he lay dead at my feet."

Tilting her head back, she lifted a hand, cupping his cheek with her palm. "I'm sorry you had to go through that, Travis."

Turning his face to kiss her palm, he refused to accept her sympathy. "Volunteering to fight for the Confederacy was something I had to do. I only regret not being home when my wife and daughter were sick. Maybe, well..." He glanced away, searching for a way to ease the guilt.

"From what I know of the illness that spread across Tennessee, there wasn't anything you could've done. Some survived it, many didn't. Your wife helped many people before she and your daughter took sick. I believe she was simply too exhausted to live through it."

"And my daughter?"

She shook her head, eyes clouding. "Too young perhaps. All I know is there are no easy answers, Travis. Why did my husband become sick and die? He may have been older than me by several years, but he still had a lot of life ahead of him. I could make myself crazy trying to make sense of something that has no answer." She glanced behind him, seeing the coffee pot sitting on the counter. "I'd better make coffee and relieve Rachel. I'm sure she would like a few minutes to rest."

Lowering himself into a chair, Travis scrubbed a hand over his face, thinking over what she'd said. He'd spent a good deal of time over the last several years blaming himself. The self-recrimination accomplished nothing, except closing him off from Isabella and a possible future with her.

"Here. You look like you need this more than me." Isabella handed him a cup of coffee. Picking up two more cups, she nodded toward the hallway. "I'm going to see if Rachel will take a little time away."

"How about I sit in there with you?"

Her mouth tilted into a relieved smile. "Thanks, Travis. I'd like that."

Isabella sat next to Travis, both watching Swift Bear's chest rise and fall. He hadn't woken since they brought Rachel coffee, encouraging her to leave the room for a spell. After a few minutes of coaxing, she did as they asked, closing the door behind her.

Touching a hand to the young Indian's head, Isabella tensed. "I'm not a nurse like Rachel, but I'm certain he's still too warm." Dipping a cloth in cool water, she placed it on his forehead. "I don't know what else we can do."

"Whenever our daughter took a fever, my wife and I would put her in a cool bath. It usually worked."

"I did the same with Jack when he was young. With the bullet wound, Rachel didn't want to risk it until the doctor gets here." She cast a frustrated glance at the door. "I wonder what's taking so long."

Travis shook his head, reaching out to take her hand. "Both Charles and Clay could be with patients. Or one may have been gone. They don't usually leave town at the same time."

A soft knock sounded before the door opened and Rachel walked in, followed by Clay McCord. Standing, Travis moved out of the way.

A hopeful look appeared on Isabella's face. "We're so glad you could come."

Setting down his bag, he placed a hand on Swift Bear's forehead. "I came as soon as I could. Charles is out at the Murton's, tending to two sick children, and Horace Clausen was at the clinic, complaining of stomach pains." Turning, Clay reached into his bag, pulling out a leather pouch. "Isabella, would you mind making a tea with this willow bark?"

"Not at all." She took it from his hand, hurrying from the room.

Shifting back to the bed, he looked at Rachel. "What is his name?"

"Swift Bear. He's the grandson of the Blackfoot chief, Running Bear."

The door burst open, Bull stepping inside. "Where is he?" His gaze shot to the bed, his features stilling. "I just got back from town and heard Swift Bear was shot."

Travis nodded to the hall. "Come with me. I'll explain what happened."

Bull didn't move. "Doc?"

Clay glanced away from examining the bullet wound. "The wound is clean and I don't see any infection, but he has a fever. Isabella is making willow bark tea. Hopefully, it will cool him off."

"Has anyone sent word to Running Bear?"

Travis shook his head. "Dax wanted to wait until you returned. You know the chief as well as anyone, and—"

"I'll go. Travis, would you mind explaining what happened while I walk over to the house to speak with Lydia? She was in town with me. I sent her to the house when I heard about Swift Bear."

"Let's go." Travis led the way out of the house toward Bull's place several yards away. As they walked, he described the hunt, the men pursuing Swift Bear, and how he was shot. "Isabella and I recognized him right away. We got him here as soon as we could."

Bull stopped, his expression haunted. "Could they be the same men who attacked us after church?"

The muscles in Travis's jaw worked. "Could've been. I didn't see much..." His voice trailed off, his mind recalling the brief moments of the shooting. "I shot one in the chest. His hat flew off." He looked at Bull. "It may still be there. I'd better go back to the spot and see what I can find."

"We'll both go, and we'll take Mal. He's a good tracker and knows Running Bear. I'll get him. Can you be ready in thirty minutes?"

Travis nodded. "I'm ready when you are."

Travis, Bull, and Mal searched the area, looking for anything the gunmen may have left behind. "I'm certain one of them lost his hat when I shot him."

"They could've grabbed it when they hauled him away." Bull looked under a group of shrubs.

"Are you certain this is the spot, Travis?" Mal knelt, looking at a disturbed patch of leaves.

"I'm sure."

Looking closer, Mal reached out, touching gouges in the dirt. "Looks like someone was dragged from here." His gaze studied the immediate area. "Over there." Standing, Mal walked to a clump of leaves covering a dark blue piece of material. "I've got something." Brushing the leaves aside, he pulled out a threadbare blue Union Army hat. "Is this what you saw?" Holding it up, he walked toward Travis.

"That's it."

Bull stared at the cap. "Didn't someone say one of the gunmen at the church wore a Union hat?"

Travis took the hat from Mal's hand. "They did." He looked at Bull. "I believe it's time Gabe got back in touch with the colonel at Fort Connall."

"You're right. You head back to Splendor, Travis, show Gabe what we found. Mal and I will continue to Running Bear's village." Bull scanned the area, then looked back at Travis.

"Are you sure you don't want me to ride along? Three are better than two, and there were at least five men chasing Swift Bear. Mal and I can then ride north to the fort and talk to the colonel directly."

Mal looked at Bull. "He has a point."

A troubled expression crossed Bull's face, then disappeared. "I suppose you're right. If you head back to town, it'll be two days before a rider could get to the fort."

Mal rubbed his chin. "It's only half a day's ride from the village to the fort."

Bull lifted his head, checking the location of the sun. "Let's ride another couple hours, then make camp. We can be at the Blackfoot village late tomorrow morning."

Travis's mouth drew into a thin line. "Be vigilant. I wouldn't mind finding the miscreants who shot Swift Bear, but we don't want to ride into a trap."

Bull lifted his gun from its holster, checking the cylinder, his features grim. "I hope we do come across them. Anyone who'd chase someone through the forest, shooting him in the back, is in need of a lesson in right and wrong."

Travis glanced at Mal, lifting a brow. "How about we figure that part out once we find them."

A grim smile curled Bull's lips. "If we come across them, Travis, I guarantee we won't have time to figure anything out. The only thing we'll have time to do is draw our guns."

"There it is. Running Bear's village." Bull stared at the mass of tents and activity below them, feeling a tug in his chest. Drawing in a breath, he tightened his hold on the reins. "We'd best get down there."

He looked behind them, not surprised to see the group of Blackfoot braves still following. They'd been back there for at least an hour, ready to move if the men showed any signs of hostility.

Travis followed Bull's gaze. "Are they going to accompany us all the way to the village?"

Bull snickered. "They always have before. I see no reason they won't this time. Let's go."

Following the well-traveled trail, they rode single file down the steep, rocky path, giving the horses their head. Bull kept them at a slow pace. It wouldn't take much for a horse to lose its footing, plummeting themselves and their riders to the bottom.

Halfway down the trail, the village burst with activity. Men stood, pointing to the hillside. Women grabbed children, rushing into their tipis and closing the flaps while the braves behind them drew closer.

"The older man standing by the tipi on the right is Running Bear." Bull lifted a hand in greeting, letting out a relieved breath when the chief returned the gesture.

Reaching the bottom of the trail, Travis and Mal stiffened when a group of young men rushed up to surround them.

Bull looked over his shoulder. "Relax. They won't do anything without Running Bear's approval." Reining to a stop several feet from the chief, Bull waited for his invitation to dismount.

"My friend, Bull Mason. It has been too long." Running Bear stepped closer, his eyes narrowing on Bull before he moved his gaze to Travis and Mal. "You have come with news, my friend. Please, get down and walk with me."

Sliding to the ground, Bull drew in a deep breath before handing the reins to one of the waiting Indians. "Stay where you are. This may take a while."

Following Running Bear, he remained silent, waiting until the chief indicated it was his turn to speak.

"My people are good here. Dax Pelletier and his brother have been generous with their cattle. We have plenty of food." Running Bear glanced at Bull. "We have peace. What of you, Bull Mason? Do you also have peace?"

Taking his time, Bull thought through his response, deciding to be honest. "No, Running Bear."

Stopping on the trail, the chief turned toward him. "Tell me."

"There has been a shooting north of Redemption's Edge. Your grandson, Swift Bear, was shot."

Running Bear's expression remained calm, his eyes widening the only indication the news surprised him. "My grandson. He lives?"

"My friend, Travis Dixon, took him to the ranch. Rachel Pelletier took care of him until the doctor arrived. He had a fever when we left, but the wound showed no infection."

"Did Swift Bear say the name of the man who shot him?"

Bull shook his head. "From what I know, he hasn't been awake long enough to say anything."

Once more, Running Bear studied Bull's face. "What of your thoughts, Bull Mason? Do you know who did this?"

Fighting the urge to take off his hat and run fingers through his hair, Bull shook his head. "What I know is not enough to be certain."

"Tell me what you know."

"We found a hat of one of the men. It's all we have to try to identify the gunmen."

Running Bear nodded, his expression grim. "Tell me of this hat."

"Wouldn't you rather go to Swift Bear? See for yourself he is all right?"

Shaking his head, he sat down on a nearby rock, resting his hands on his knees. "I will go to my grandson. First, tell me of this hat."

Grimacing, Bull's mouth twisted. "It's a soldier's hat, Running Bear."

His brows lifted. "From the fort?"

"I don't know. Travis and Mal will go speak with the leader of Fort Connall. Perhaps he will recognize it."

Nodding, Running Bear's gaze moved over the clearing around them, giving away nothing about his thoughts.

"Have you met the colonel?"

The chief took a moment before nodding. "I have met the tall man who leads the fort. He is a hard man."

Bull cocked his head to the side. "How do you know this?"

A pained expression formed on the chief's face. "I rode with a hunting party. Swift Bear was with us. We came across a group of soldiers led by this colonel." He looked at Bull. "Colonel McArthur."

Bull waited, not wanting to interrupt Running Bear's thoughts. When the silence continued, he took a step closer. "And?"

"His men surrounded us, kept us there to watch."

"Watch what?"

Standing, Running Bear moved past him toward the village. "He killed two of his men."

228

Chapter Seventeen

Fort Connall

Sliding from his horse, Travis's gaze moved around the inside of the fort, noting the number of horses in the stable, store, barracks, and stockade. He stopped on the last, seeing a pair of hands gripping the bars, a dirty face staring out.

Bull had shared what Running Bear said about the colonel's actions, wondering about the circumstances. During the war, Travis knew the man by reputation. They were both cavalry officers, which meant the odds were good they'd faced each other in battle.

"I'm Captain Ryerson. May I help you, gentlemen?"

Travis reached into his shirt, pulling out the cap they'd found in the woods. "A group of us were hunting along Wildfire Creek a few days ago. A boy was shot by someone wearing this cap. Do you recognize it?"

Jonah grabbed the hat from Travis's hand, turning it over. "Most of our men own a cap like this one."

"We need to find the soldier who lost it."

Settling clenched hands on his hips, Jonah's gaze narrowed. "Why do you think he'd be here at Fort Connall? It could be anyone."

"It could be, but I'm thinking the group of men who chased the boy and shot him came from right here."

Shifting his weight, Jonah looked toward the colonel's office, then back at Travis. "Is that your gut talking, or do you have proof?"

"A few weeks ago, a group of men attacked our town, killing one man and injuring a couple others outside the church. According to one person, at least one wore a uniform. A few days ago, a group of men chase and shoot a boy, leaving this cap behind. You want to believe it's my gut, that's fine. All I know is our sheriff, Gabe Evans, asked for help from your colonel and he refused."

Jonah shook his head. "We're short men."

During the war, a comment like that most often referred to men deserting their posts.

Travis crossed his arms, his features a mask. "Meaning you have deserters."

Nostrils flaring, Jonah glared at him. "I mean exactly as I said. We're short men."

Travis shot a look at Mal, who shook his head. "Look, Captain, I don't know the reasons for hiding the fact you've got a group of deserters raiding these parts. All I know is they're dangerous and don't care who they kill. They wounded a child, killed a good man, and shot Chief Running Bear's grandson."

Jonah's eyes widened. "The Blackfoot chief?"

A muscle in Travis's jaw twitched. Drawing in a deep breath, he gave a curt nod.

Jonah's hands fisted at his sides. "Damn those men." Lips slipping into a thin line, his gaze moved to the colonel's office. "Wait here."

Rubbing his chin, Travis looked at Mal. "I wonder how long those men have been gone."

Disgust distorted Mal's face. "Long enough to end at least one life."

"And maybe start a war with the Blackfoot."

Mal shook his head. "Running Bear doesn't want war."

"Maybe not now. He may change his mind if Swift Bear doesn't make it."

"Are you men from Splendor?" They turned to see a tall, square-shouldered man wearing a colonel's insignia stop before them. "I'm Colonel McArthur." He didn't hold out his hand, and neither offered theirs.

Travis crossed his arms, giving the leader of Fort Connall a long stare. "I believe it's time we came to an understanding, Colonel."

Dax dropped the pen on another Army contract he'd been trying to read for almost thirty minutes, disgusted with the ease at which he became distracted. Recent events held a spot in his mind and he couldn't shake them. The church shooting, Swift Bear's wound, the men chasing him, and the way the colonel at Fort Connall ignored their plight provoked a tightness in his throat he couldn't push aside.

In his heart, he knew the men who attacked the town were the same ones who shot Swift Bear. Dax's gut told him they were connected to the fort and warned him the danger wasn't over.

"Bull is back, and Running Bear is with him." Dax glanced up, seeing Dirk standing in the doorway. "There are five other Blackfoot with them."

Pushing up, Dax grabbed his hat, leaving his gunbelt on its hook. "Would you mind letting Rachel and Isabella know he's here?"

Dirk nodded, walking down the hall to the first bedroom. Tapping on the door, he opened it. "How's Swift Bear doing?"

Rachel pursed her lips. "His fever is gone. He wakes long enough to drink some broth, then falls back to sleep." She shook her head. "We've asked how he's feeling, but he never responds."

"He might now. Bull is back, and he has Running Bear with him. You should be prepared for him."

"Thanks, Dirk." Isabella picked up a cloth, dipping it into the basin and wringing it out. "I'll mop away the dampness if you'll straighten the bedding."

"Do you need any help from me?"

Rachel glanced at the door, forgetting Dirk still stood in the room. "We're fine, thanks. Is Lydia still here?"

He gave a small smile. "If she's the one cooking, the wonderful smells coming from the kitchen tell me she is."

"Yes, that's Lydia. Would you let her know Bull and the chief are here?"

Dirk nodded. "If Bull hasn't already beaten me to it." He shut the door behind him.

Wiping her hands on a dry cloth, Rachel took one more look at Swift Bear. "The wound is healing and there's no fever." She let out a breath. "Perhaps seeing Running Bear will help."

Sharp raps on the door drew their attention. "Running Bear is here. May we come in?"

Rachel's face lit up at her husband's voice. Opening the door, she smiled at him. "Please, come in." She and Dax both stepped aside, allowing Running Bear to enter first.

The Blackfoot chief gave a curt nod to Rachel, then Isabella, before his gaze moved to the bed. His grandson lay on his left side.

Rachel walked the few paces to stop next to him. "Doctor McCord was able to get Swift Bear's fever down. The gunshot wound is healing."

Running Bear looked at her, his face devoid of all emotion. "Does my grandson speak?"

She shook her head. "When he wakes, he mumbles a little before falling back to sleep. He has taken some broth, but nothing else."

Giving a low grunt, Running Bear turned to Dax. "We will take him to the village now."

"Are you certain you want to move him?" Rachel asked before Dax could voice a response. The chief slowly turned his face toward hers, meeting her gaze, his features unreadable. "I mean, wouldn't you like to stay the night to see how he does?" She glanced at Dax, silently asking for his support. He lifted a brow, shrugging. Biting her lower lip, she looked back at Running Bear. "The doctor will be back this afternoon to check on his progress. I know you want him home as soon as possible, but it might be wise to wait a little longer."

Something in Running Bear's gaze caught her attention, but he didn't respond. Instead, he turned to Dax. "Your woman speaks for you, Dax Pelletier?"

Shooting a quick look at Rachel, Dax held his grin. "In matters regarding sickness and injury, yes. Rachel worked as a nurse in Union field hospitals during the war. I'll wager she has more experience than many doctors when it comes to gunshot wounds."

Running Bear gave a short nod, turning back to Rachel. "Then it will be as you say. We will wait for your doctor. Tomorrow, we will take Swift Bear back to his mother."

"Neither his mother nor father came with you?" If either of her boys had been shot, no one would've been able to keep her away.

The chief's face clouded, signaling she may have overstepped her bounds. Moving his gaze to the bed, he shook his head. "His father died when Swift Bear was young. His mother is with child. Her time is too near to travel this distance."

Hands clasped in front of her, Rachel's tension eased. "Would you like to sit in here for a while? Maybe seeing you will help him." She indicated a chair next to the bed. "We will give you some privacy." Looking at Isabella and Dax, she nodded toward the door.

"Rachel Pelletier?"

"Yes, Running Bear?"

"Thank you."

The day grew late with no sign of Clay. Running Bear had left the bedroom once to summon all but two of his men into the house. Isabella and Lydia provided food, getting short nods of thanks before shutting the door behind them.

"I wish Clay would arrive." Rachel held baby James while Patrick played in a corner of Dax's study.

"He'll be here. If he can't come, he'll send your uncle. Who I worry about is Travis and Mal." Dax sat at his desk, glancing out the window toward the barn. "They should've been back by now."

Shifting James to her other hip, Rachel thought of Isabella. She knew her friend was worried Travis would come across the group of men who'd shot Swift Bear. "Perhaps they were able to talk the colonel into looking for the men. Knowing Mal and Travis, they would've volunteered to ride with them."

The front door burst open, boots pounding toward the study before Dirk looked in. "A rider is coming from town."

"Doctor McCord?"

He shook his head. "Not the doctor. Looks like Mack, Gabe's deputy. He's coming in as if the devil is after him."

Dax stood, grabbing his gunbelt and strapping it around his waist. "Until I find out what Mack wants, keep everyone in the house, Rachel." Not waiting for her response, he followed Dirk outside.

Mack Mackey had been in Splendor almost a year. He and Caleb Covington were both majors in the Union Army, serving under Gabe. The town was fortunate to have them serving as deputies under their former commander.

Mack didn't slow his horse until a few yards from the house. Reining hard, he jumped off. "The gunmen came back, Dax. The gang got in and out of the bank before anyone could stop them, then shot up the town. Their bullets went right through windows, hitting a couple ranch hands in the Dixie and a man who'd come in on the stage." Mack let out a disgusted breath. "They took off this way." He looked past Dax, seeing Rachel, Isabella, and Lydia peering out the front window. "Gabe wanted me to warn you."

"How are the people they shot?"

"Alive. We got them to the clinic."

Dax clasped him on the shoulder. "Thanks, Mack. Go inside, get something to drink."

Mack shook his head. "Can't. Gabe needs me back in town."

Dax's gaze moved about the group of men who'd gathered around. "Tat and Johnny, go with Mack."

"If you don't mind, I'd like to go, Dax." Dirk stepped next to him, his face ashen. "I want to make sure Rosemary is all right."

Dax nodded. "Of course. Tat, you'll be riding with Dirk and Mack."

"Yes, sir," he responded, taking off to saddle his horse.

"They should stay with you, Dax."

"We're good, Mack. I don't want you riding out alone, maybe running into that group of killers. Truth is, I wouldn't be able to keep Dirk here with Rosemary working at the clinic. Can anyone describe the men's clothing, hats...anything?"

"Harold Clausen got a real good look. So did a couple others who were in the bank. Noah came running out of the livery as they rode past. He said three of them wore Union caps and shirts. Another had a feather sticking out of a headband."

"Could Noah tell if he was Crow?"

Mack shook his head. "He didn't get that good a look." His eyes took on a hard gleam. "Damn that Colonel McArthur."

Dax rubbed his jaw. Travis and Mal had ridden to the fort. He sure wished they had this information before talking to the colonel.

"Well, we can't wait for help from Fort Connall. I'll get the men positioned around the area. Don't send Tat back until you're sure there's no more danger. Dirk will ride back when he's ready."

"They'd be fools to ride back in again, Dax."

Snorting, he shook his head. "I'm afraid fools are what we're dealing with, Mack."

Watching Mack, Dirk, and Tat ride off, Dax shifted his gaze to the front window, shaking his head at the question he saw in Rachel's eyes. He now knew why Clay hadn't made it to the ranch.

"I've got the men positioned with plenty of ammunition, Dax." Bull shot a look at Lydia, who stood inside. "What about the women and children?"

"Get them all upstairs, and give the women guns." Pulling out his revolver, he checked the cylinder. "I need to speak with Running Bear."

"I'll do it. You need to let Luke and Ginny know what's happened."

Letting out a harsh oath, Dax nodded. "He's working one of the wild horses at his place." He glanced around, his gaze landing on Billy Zales, one of the orphans who worked at the ranch. "I'll have Billy ride over."

"Sam should go with him." Bull spotted Lydia's brother checking a rifle near the corner of the barn. "I know Sam and Billy are almost grown, but I'd rather see them away from here if that group of outlaws comes this way."

"I don't know if they'll be any better off at Luke's." Dax rubbed the back of his neck. "The three-way fork north of town leads them here, to Luke's, or east of both our places. Still, Luke needs to know what happened."

Bull's hands fisted at his sides. "If those boys have a smidgen of sense, they'll go east, as far away from us as they can get."

"I'm afraid that's a lot to hope for. I'll let Billy and Sam know while you're inside." Dax started to turn away, then stopped. "And don't let Rachel argue with you. She needs to be upstairs with everyone else."

Bull headed up the front steps, mumbling something about always getting the impossible jobs.

Chapter Eighteen

Splendor

"Do you remember your name?" Clay McCord leaned over the patient, checking the wound to the left side of his head. Getting no response, he opened the man's eyes, looking at his pupils. "Half an inch to the right and you'd be dead."

He received the same response as when Beau and Cash carried the man into the clinic. Nothing. Clay hadn't expected one, not with the wound cutting a path through his thick, dark hair. He guessed the man would be out for several hours, which would be a blessing, as there were two others requiring help. Thank goodness Doc Worthington had returned from delivering a baby. Otherwise, Clay and Rosemary would be dealing with all three patients.

Pulling the blanket under the man's chin, Clay walked out, going to the room of another victim. "How's he doing, Rosemary?"

"No fever. He hasn't woken up since passing out when you removed the bullet." She touched the young man's forehead, brushing away damp strands of hair. "I don't believe he's more than seventeen. Have you ever seen him before?"

Clay shook his head. "I've never seen any of the three that were brought in today. I do know the one in the suit got off the stage not long before the outlaws rode through. Beau said he thought the two ranch hands worked for the same brand, but didn't say who." He leaned down, checking the patient's pulse and his pupils, then straightened. "Well, I'd better see how Charles is doing with the other one. Fetch me when he wakes up."

"Of course, Doctor." Sliding a chair next to the bed, she sat down for the first time since the shooting.

Rosemary had been putting away supplies when she'd heard gunfire. Rushing to the window, she'd leaned out, seeing riders dashing toward the north end of town. Her heart rate picked up a moment later when several men, including Beau and Cash, carried the victims between buildings to the clinic.

This wasn't the first time she'd been glad the new two-story building stood on the back street. The location provided more protection than the original clinic and reduced the amount of dust common on the main street.

Hearing heavy footfalls on the stairs, she started to rise when the door burst open.

"Rosemary..." Dirk's relieved voice breathed out. Moving close, he pulled her up, wrapping his arms around her. "Are you all right?"

Smiling against his chest, she nodded. "I'm fine, Dirk. I was in the clinic when the men rode through town." Dropping her arms from around his waist, her gaze shifted to the patient. "Three men were shot. This is one of them."

Not wanting to let her go, he settled an arm over her shoulders. "Will he recover?"

"If he avoids infection, he should be all right. The bullet lodged in his chest, but Doctor McCord removed it. A few inches and it would have hit a lung. His friend was shot in the leg. Another bullet grazed the left side of the third man's head. The doctor thinks he'll be fine in a few days. It isn't good, but better than anyone being killed."

He didn't answer. Moving to the window, he scanned the street, his gaze landing on Gabe and Cash. "I'm going to speak with Gabe. Are you going to be all right?"

"I'm safe in the clinic, Dirk. Please don't worry about me."

"That's never going to happen." Leaning down, he kissed her cheek. "When I leave, you're riding back to the ranch with me."

"I don't know how long I'll need to stay."

Stroking her hair, he placed one more kiss on her lips. "Don't argue about this, Rosemary.

Charles and Clay live in town and can keep watch on the men. You're riding back with me."

Redemption's Edge

"They got away with twice as much from the bank as last time, shot three men, then rode off. Beau and Cash tried to track them, but lost their trail the same as last time." Dirk took a sip of the whiskey Dax handed him, rolling the glass between his fingers. Looking out the window, he watched the sun sink over the western mountains. "Damn long day," he murmured.

"What's that?"

Dirk shook his head. "Gabe and the deputies, along with Noah, Nick, and Baron Klaussner are on watch, but Gabe doesn't think they'll hit the bank a third time. He's pretty sure they'll get away from here now that they have a good amount of cash."

Dax cocked a brow. "Baron Klaussner?"

"Ernst refused to stay in the hotel and do nothing. Gabe positioned him in the lobby, which seemed to satisfy the baron. Gabe did refuse to let his father be involved." A slight smile curled Dirk's lips. "He sent Walter back to the house to keep watch on Lena and Jack."

Dax ran a hand along the edge of his desk, then stood. "I sent Billy and Sam to Luke's. Wyatt is going to bring Nora back here in the morning. He doesn't want her staying in town."

"Do you think we're any safer here?"

"No, I don't. We do have Running Bear and his men. They know what happened and will help if the outlaws attack. I have to agree with Gabe. The gang is going to ride as far away from here as they can. They won't take a chance on getting away a third time."

Hearing a noise out front, Dax walked to the window. "Well, I'll be damned."

Dirk joined him, looking outside, a grin crossing his face. "It looks like Travis brought the cavalry."

"Let Running Bear know while I greet our guests." Dax started for the door, stopping when it swung open.

"Did you see who's here?" Rachel nodded toward the front.

"I know. I'd appreciate it if you'd stay upstairs with the children."

"But, Dax—"

Catching her chin with his fingers, he turned her face up to his. "Just because Travis arrived with Colonel McArthur doesn't mean we're safe. Your safety is my most important concern. Please stay upstairs with the others until I find out what's going on." Kissing her, Dax dropped his hand, not taking his eyes from hers.

The fight left her at the concern on his face. "All right," she breathed out, then smiled. "But don't make me wait up there too long."

"Wouldn't think of it." Dax opened the door, almost crashing into Travis as he bounded up the steps.

"Isabella?"

"She's upstairs." Dax grabbed Travis's arm before he could move past him. "She's fine. Tell me what McArthur is doing here."

"He came to see Running Bear. The colonel is worried the shooting of Swift Bear will spark a war."

Dax flicked a look at McArthur. "Running Bear doesn't want war, but he does want the men who shot his grandson punished. There's something else."

"What?"

"There's been another attack on the town. Three men were shot after the outlaws robbed the bank."

Travis fisted his hands at his sides. "Did they find them?"

"No. The gang rode north out of town. Beau and Cash tried to pick up the trail, but lost them.

That's why I've got all except a few men here, in case those bandits find their way to the ranch."

"Mr. Pelletier?"

Dax turned to see the leader of Fort Connall walking up the steps.

"Yes."

"I'm Colonel Miles McArthur."

Accepting the outstretched hand, Dax nodded toward the house. "I've been told you're here to see Running Bear."

"And inquire as to the condition of his grandson. Is he alive?"

A man who didn't waste time. Dax could respect that. "He is. Running Bear and one of his men are with him. The others are over there." He turned his gaze to the other side of the barn where several Blackfoot openly stared at the soldiers. "It wasn't easy to get the chief to agree to stay the night. He wanted to take his grandson back to the village today."

The front door opened, Dirk moving aside to allow Running Bear to walk past him and onto the porch. The chief stopped, taking several moments to study the colonel, his features indicating nothing of what he thought.

"Chief Running Bear. I am Colonel McArthur from Fort Connall. I met you one other time."

"I know who you are, Colonel McArthur." Before him stood the man Running Bear witnessed shooting his own men. The chief wondered about the reasons for the killings.

"I've come to ask about your grandson."

Running Bear's eyes flashed for an instant, then stilled. "He lives. Have you found the men who shot him?"

"We aren't sure who they are."

Travis stepped forward. "I beg your pardon, Colonel. It's my understanding you do know who shot Swift Bear and shot up Splendor this morning."

Miles shifted to face him. "There were more shootings in town?"

"This morning." Dax's voice held a dangerous edge. "The same group of men who attacked us at church came back, robbed the bank, and shot three men. That's a total of one dead and six shot, including Swift Bear. Don't you think it's time you told us what you've been hiding?"

"I'm still not certain the men who attacked Splendor are the deserters from Fort Connall. It's been weeks since they rode out on patrol and never returned." Miles sat in the study with Dax, Travis, Wyatt, Bull, Dirk, and Running Bear after finishing the best meal he had in a long time. Cradling his glass of whiskey in his palms, he leaned forward. "Their leader, Sergeant Dowling, is as ruthless as anyone I've ever known. Our Crow scout, Black Feather, was with him and three other soldiers plus two civilians when they disappeared."

Running Bear's brow lifted. "I know this Crow...Black Feather." He looked at Bull. "He is from Red Tail's village."

Bull's nostrils flared, jaw tightening at the mention of the Crow chief who'd kidnapped Lydia.

Miles saw the silent exchange, wondering what had happened between the Crow and Bull. "Black Feather was paid as an Army scout. Leaving his post is the same transgression as any soldier who deserts." Only one man in the room displayed confusion. "The punishment for desertion is death by firing squad, Running Bear."

The chief gave a curt nod, finally understanding what he'd witnessed months before when first meeting the colonel.

Dax crossed his arms, resting a hip against the edge of his desk. "Do you know why they'd stay around here and not get as far away as they could?"

"Money. They couldn't have had much when they left. When Captain Ryerson collected their personal belongings, he found letters, pictures, money...items they would've taken if they'd known they were leaving." Miles took another sip of whiskey, letting the amber liquid burn a path down his throat.

"You think Sergeant Dowling threatened them into leaving?" Travis asked.

The colonel shrugged. "Possibly. Or they saw an opportunity and took it. From what you've told me about the two raids on your town, I believe they robbed the bank the first time a few days after leaving the fort."

Dax's eyes lit with anger. "Yet you refused help when Gabe asked for it, and didn't tell him you had a group of deserters."

Miles didn't flinch at his bitter tone. "I made the best decision for my men."

"But not for the people of Splendor."

"As the commander of the fort, I have obligations, Mr. Pelletier."

"I'm well aware of command obligations, Colonel." Straightening, Dax paced several feet away, then rounded on Miles. "You also have an obligation to the civilians in your region when asked for assistance. At the very least, you should've gotten word to Gabe about the deserters so he could've been prepared."

Standing, Miles stalked to within a couple feet of Dax. "I had no idea they'd be so stupid as to raid a town."

Dax refused to back down. "Even when you *knew* they had little money and food? They were desperate, with only one bank close enough to rob. Common sense would've told any reasonable man where they'd be headed."

Miles moved to within inches of Dax's chest. "Are you insinuating I'm a fool?"

"I'm stating a fact. If you don't like it, maybe you'd better change your thinking."

Seeing Miles move his hand to the handle of his gun, Bull jumped between the two men, shoving them apart.

"That's enough!"

Dax fought the urge to shove Bull aside. Scrubbing a hand down his face, he turned away, swearing loud enough for anyone standing outside the study to hear.

Bull settled clenched hands on his hips. "This isn't going to help us find those men."

"They're long gone." Everyone's attention shifted to Dirk. "The colonel already admitted all they needed was money before getting as far away from here as possible. Beau and Cash couldn't find their tracks. My guess is they're already in Big Pine or on their way to Moosejaw. 'Course, they could've ridden south to Wyoming or southwest to Utah."

Shredding a hand through his hair, Travis looked at Dax. "I'm thinking the same as Dirk. It makes no sense they'd stay around. Those men aren't going to take the chance."

Dax shifted his gaze. "Bull?"

Staring down at the floor, he let out a frustrated breath. "I've gotta say, I agree with Dirk and Travis."

His gaze moved to the last of his men. "Wyatt?"

"Those outlaws are gone, boss. I'm guessing they rode north to throw us off, then turned south to Wyoming."

Pinching the bridge of his nose, Dax stalked to his desk, settling into his chair before looking at Miles. "What are your intentions?"

"I plan to find their trail and catch them. You say they robbed the bank this morning?"

Dax nodded. "That's right."

"I believe there's a good chance Dowling and his crew will make camp for the night. That's when we'll find them." Miles turned his attention to Running Bear. The chief had yet to utter a word since the heated debate started. "You know this territory. Where would you go if you were them?"

Standing, the chief crossed his arms, his eyes locked on the colonel. "I would follow Black Feather."

"And where would Black Feather lead them?"

Running Bear thought a moment, his mouth curling into a wry grin. "Wolf Creek Mountain."

Bull's brows furrowed. "That's northeast of here. I've heard rumors the mountain has mystical powers. Why would he take them there to find a safe hiding place?"

Running Bear's eyes softened, looking at a man he thought of as a friend. "Black Feather is not taking them there to hide, Bull Mason. He is taking them to their deaths."

Chapter Nineteen

Travis stood on the porch watching the sunrise, his arm around Isabella's waist. The contentment on their faces indicated neither cared if anyone thought their closeness inappropriate.

Sipping the cup of coffee in his other hand, he watched Miles roust his men for the trip north. They would accompany Running Bear until the trail split toward the Blackfoot village. He and his men would continue north, veering east, past the fort to Wolf Creek Mountain.

Travis had also heard the same rumors as Bull. Stories of strange happenings, mythical beings, and people climbing the mountain, never to be seen again. He'd ignored them, never having met anyone who'd actually been to one of the most rugged mountains in the territory.

"Do you think they'll find them?"

He finished the last of his coffee, letting out a breath. "I don't know."

"Dax told Rachel what Running Bear said."

Travis chuckled. "Let me guess. Rachel told you."

Isabella gave a self-satisfied nod. "Yes, she did. And I told Lydia." She leaned into him. "Do you believe what the chief said?"

His lips drew into a thin line, thinking about Running Bear's prediction. "It's possible. Black Feather is a Crow and they've long believed in the strange powers of Wolf Creek Mountain."

"Is that why the chief believes he's taking them to their deaths?"

Travis wondered the same. It made no sense for Black Feather to take them into the mystical mountain where he'd be as likely to die as them. He'd heard nothing of the Crow being immune to the strange, and possibly deadly, powers.

"I don't believe so."

"Then why?"

"Running Bear didn't share his reasons with us."

Isabella lifted her head, staring up at him. "Travis, I'm asking what *you* think."

"Pure greed."

Her features scrunched together, eyes narrowing. "Greed?"

"Black Feather has come to embrace the white man's world. The outlaws robbed the bank twice. I don't know the amount they took, but the total is substantial. Wolf Creek Mountain is in the middle of Crow lands. My guess is he's taking them there knowing his people will kill them."

Her lips parted, eyes widening. "And he'll keep all the money."

"His village won't know the worth. They'll keep the horses, saddles, weapons, and anything else of value." Travis paused as one of the Blackfoot braves placed Swift Bear in his grandfather's arms. Running Bear would ride the entire way holding his grandson. "The money will go to Black Feather."

"And he'll share it with no one…"

"Because the outlaws who stole it will all be dead."

Placing a hand over her mouth, she did her best to hide a chuckle.

Travis's mouth twisted into a grin. "It isn't funny."

Shaking her head, she couldn't help the spark in her eyes. "No, it isn't. But there's still some type of perverse justice to it all, don't you think?"

"If that's what happens, then yes. Death is what they deserve. I don't care how it happens, as long as other innocent people don't get hurt along the way."

Isabella's breath caught when Colonel McArthur swung into his saddle. "Aren't the soldiers putting themselves in danger by going to the mountain?"

"They are, but that's their job, sweetheart. Sergeant Dowling and his men are deserters. If Colonel McArthur captures them, they'll be shot."

"Albert dead and six people wounded. For what? A little bit of money." She sighed, resting her head against his shoulder. "None of it makes sense to me, Travis."

He had no response. So much in his life didn't make sense.

Neither spoke as Running Bear and his braves rode past, followed by Colonel McArthur and his men. Faces solemn, their gazes fixed straight ahead, not one gave even the slightest nod to those watching them leave.

"I certainly hope Running Bear is right about the deserters going to Wolf Creek Mountain." Bull walked up the porch steps. "My instincts say otherwise, but they've been wrong before."

"How often?" Travis asked.

Bull offered a wry grin. "Not very."

"What do your instincts say this time?"

He stared at the retreating group of riders, then looked at Travis. "If it were me, I'd stay far away from Wolf Creek Mountain and head south. Wyoming, Utah, maybe even Arizona. Riding north makes no sense, unless they've put all their faith in Black Feather." He waited until Dax and Wyatt joined them. "What do you think, Dax?"

"I'd do the same, Bull. Then again, we don't think the same as a band of killers." Dax glanced at the men still stationed around the barn and house, rifles at the ready. "We'll keep our defenses up until we hear back from Colonel McArthur. He agreed to let us know if they find the deserters. Bull, let Dirk know we'll keep the current number of men with the herd for a few more days."

"I'm going to take Nora back to town, Dax."

"That's your decision, Wyatt. She's welcome to stay here as long as she wants."

"I appreciate it, boss. Allie needs her at the shop, and I agree with you and Bull. Wherever those vermin are, they've left Splendor behind. Nora's going to stay with Gabe and Lena for a few nights so I can be here at the ranch."

"You don't need to do that, Wyatt."

"I want to, Dax. With the number of men posted as guards, you need me here. Gabe won't let anything happen to her."

Dax grasped Wyatt's shoulder. "Stay vigilant."

"I will. I'll get Nora and we'll be on our way. See you in a couple hours."

Travis dropped his arm from around Isabella's waist, shifting toward Dax. "Do you want me to ride over to Luke's and let him know what's happening?"

"I'd appreciate it. Let him know we're fine here if he wants to stay to work on those mares he cut from the wild herd."

"I'll go back with you, Travis."

His body stilled at Isabella's words. Taking a slow breath, he turned back to her. "I'd rather you stay here. I won't be gone long."

Clasping her hands together, she lifted her chin. "Ginny might need help with Cooper, and it's time Rachel and Dax got their house back."

Dax shook his head. "You don't have to leave, Isabella. We've plenty of room, and I know Rachel enjoys your company."

"Thank you, Dax. I'll speak with Ginny. If she doesn't need my help, I'll return with Travis." She glanced down at the dress Rachel had loaned her. "Regardless, I do need a change of clothes. All I have are the pants and shirts I took on the hunt."

"If you insist on going, then get what you need. I'll saddle our horses so we can leave as soon as you're ready." Travis hurried down the steps, long, purposeful strides taking him into the barn.

She bit her bottom lip, looking up at Dax. "I don't think he likes the idea of me going with him."

His mouth curved upward. "I don't think he's happy with you leaving at all. Come on inside and we'll let Rachel know you're going to Luke's."

Isabella stepped in front of Dax, taking a quick look over her shoulder to see Travis walk out of the barn and toward the corral with two harnesses. If she wasn't mistaken, his warm features of earlier that morning had transformed into a deep scowl.

Travis stomped to the corral, muttering to himself about his reaction to Isabella wanting to return to Luke's. It annoyed him that his chest tightened when she'd made the announcement. She'd lived with Luke and Ginny, helping with Cooper, since not long after arriving in Splendor. It was her home, not a guest room at Dax's.

Whistling for Banjo, his features softened when Isabella's mare followed the gelding toward him. They'd become attached over the last few days. The thought stilled his motions for a few moments, reminding him of how he'd become accustomed to seeing Isabella each night and every morning since they left on the hunting trip.

Travis wasn't prepared for her to return to Luke's, where he'd see her once or twice a week and at church on Sundays. The dilemma smacked him in the face. He lived in the bunkhouse, had little savings, and owned fewer possessions. He didn't want to live without her, but saw no way to live with her.

Slipping one of the harnesses on Blossom, the other on Banjo, he led them to the barn, the true nature of his life punctuating every step. He'd been so intent on first pushing her away, then regaining her trust, Travis failed to recognize he no longer owned a farm, had no place to live if they married. The Pelletiers paid well, but not enough to support Isabella and a family. Offering her marriage without children would never work.

Beads of sweat rose on his forehead, and they weren't from the exertion of saddling the horses. Now that he'd accepted how much he loved and needed her, Travis had to face an ugly reality he couldn't take care of Isabella.

"I'm ready."

The sound of her voice always lightened his mood. Today, it brought the pain of truth. "I'm almost ready." He finished cinching Blossom's saddle, letting out a slow breath. No longer able to put off facing her, he turned, a pain unlike anything he'd ever felt piercing his chest.

"Travis? Are you all right?" Isabella moved to him, her hand cupping his cheek. "You look pale."

Swallowing the ball of ice lodged in his throat, he nodded. "I'm fine. In a hurry to get over to Luke's and back." Grabbing Blossom's reins, he held them out to Isabella. "I'll help you up."

Raising a brow, she stared at him a moment before taking the reins. "Thank you."

Putting his hands on her waist, he waited until she'd slipped her left boot into the stirrup, then lifted. Isabella settled easily into the saddle.

While inside, she'd changed back into her pants and shirt, finding them more comfortable than the skirt she usually wore for riding.

"Do you think Allie could sew a pair of pants and a shirt I could use for riding?"

Travis swung into Banjo's saddle, reining him around. Knowing she'd spoken but failing to hear the words, he gave her an uncomprehending stare.

"Pants, Travis."

His mouth twisted. "Pants?" He used his spurs to move Banjo out of the barn, knowing she'd follow.

"Yes. Do you think Allie could sew me a pair of pants and a shirt? These are so much more comfortable than wearing a skirt."

His mind raced with what to do about the two of them, and she was asking about clothes. "Sure."

"That's what I thought. She's so talented, and I know she sews pants for Cash. It shouldn't be hard for her to make them for women."

Travis couldn't recall the last time she'd prattled on about a topic more suited for a conversation between women. Why did she have to pick this morning when he couldn't get his mind off how much he loved her and how little he had to offer?

Taking the trail toward Luke's, he tried to think about anything except the conversation he didn't want to have. As much as he disliked the man, Travis began to wonder if Arnott had suggested she and David marry. Her late husband never would've suggested someone who couldn't support Isabella, give her the same life she'd grown accustomed to.

The same as Beau's wife, Caro, Isabella didn't need a man to support her, but she wasn't the type of woman to grow old without a husband and children. She deserved both. Beau wasn't wealthy to the same degree as Caro, but he did have an inheritance. Travis had less than nothing and no prospects for anything different in the future.

He didn't consider himself an overly bright man, but even he could predict the outcome of a marriage between him and Isabella. She'd eventually tire of a life without, living on what he made at the ranch. Because under no circumstances would he live on money earned by another man.

A tired breath escaped him when Luke's house came into view. His stomach roiled at what had to come. Travis's father had told him many times to take care of the inevitable instead of trying to put it off. Doing so only caused more problems, and sometimes more pain.

He'd never understood his father's words so completely until now.

Approaching the house, Travis spotted Luke working with one of the mares in a nearby corral. He stopped when he saw them rein up.

"Good morning, Travis, Isabella. What are you doing here?"

"Dax wants you to know what's going on with the outlaws." Travis slid to the ground, then helped Isabella down. "Do you have a few minutes?"

"As much time as you need." Luke motioned to one of his ranch hands to take care of their horses.

"I'm going inside to see Ginny and Cooper."

Watching Isabella walk away, his heart dropped into his stomach. The determination he felt not ten minutes before shifted to doubt, which was something he couldn't consider. After today, nothing would be the same. Not for Isabella, and not for him.

"I'd like to get back to the ranch as soon as possible. Can we talk out here?"

"Sure, Travis. Let's go into the barn and get out of this heat."

Grabbing a canteen hanging from a peg inside, Luke handed it to Travis. Taking a long pull, he handed it back, then sat down on a bench next to the tack room.

Swallowing several gulps, Luke hung the canteen back on its hook. Grabbing a stool, he dragged it next to Travis.

"You said there's news on the robbers."

Over the next several minutes, Travis filled him in, ending with Running Bear taking his grandson home and the soldiers riding to Wolf Creek Mountain.

Rubbing the back of his neck, Luke thought through what he'd learned. "I've never been to the mountain, so I can't speak about it with any authority. From what I've heard, it's in the middle of Crow territory, not a place most white men want to go."

"And the rumors about it?"

Luke's eyes sparked with amusement. "You mean being full of spirits and whatnot?"

Travis nodded.

"I've heard about them, but never met anyone who witnessed any spells or mystical powers. Some say it's where Crow spirits live out their days. I've heard others talk about people riding up the mountain and never returning. If that's what happens to those killers, I'm all for it."

"You and everyone else. Colonel McArthur will send word to Dax about what they find."

Luke reached over to a nearby stack of hay, pulling a strand out and sticking it into his mouth. "With luck, they'll find bodies to haul back to the fort."

"There are no guarantees they've ridden north. The gang could've gone south, which is what several of us believe."

"Either way, they're gone from here. I'm sure Gabe has already sent telegrams to Big Pine and Moosejaw. Probably down to Wyoming and other parts they might go. Have you heard any more about the last three men they shot?"

"Nope. Wyatt took Nora back to town. I'm sure he'll know more when he gets back. Are you all right here, or do you need Dax to send some men over?"

"We're fine here, Travis. I have two more mares to break, then I'll bring the group over and join them with the ones you and Wyatt have been working."

Standing, Travis stretched his arms above his head. "I'd better head back."

Luke pushed up, tossing the piece of hay onto the ground. "Do you want to say goodbye to Isabella before you go?"

Shoving aside the burning desire to say yes, he shook his head. "She's in with Ginny and the baby. I don't want to disturb her." Walking to Banjo, he grabbed the reins and swung into the saddle. "Send word if you need help." Fighting the urge to glance at the house, he touched Banjo with his spurs and headed out.

Travis felt a sharp pang of guilt, knowing Isabella would be confused and disappointed by him leaving without a word. He had a lot to think through before speaking to her again. Most of all, there was a conversation he had to have, and as he'd learned growing up, there was no better time than now.

Chapter Twenty

Splendor

Rosemary touched the damp cloth to the patient's forehead, feeling him flinch before a moan escaped his lips. He hadn't woken for more than a few minutes since being grazed on the left side of the head during the bank robbery.

Until earlier this morning, they didn't know his identity. Exasperated, Doc Worthington had gone through the man's jacket, discovering a Pinkerton badge and a trade card bearing the name Joel Eastman, Pinkerton Agent. Charles took the items and headed straight to the jail.

It didn't take long for Dutch McFarlin, a deputy and former Pinkerton agent, to return to the clinic with the doctor. By the time another ten minutes passed, Dutch had sent a telegram to Allan Pinkerton, letting him know of the agent's injury and requesting information on the nature of his trip to Splendor. Thinking back to the telegram he'd sent to Pinkerton about David Peeler, Dutch didn't believe Joel showing up in town was a coincidence.

Wringing the cloth out in a bowl next to the bed, Rosemary startled when Joel spoke through a parched throat. "Water..."

"You're awake, Mr. Eastman."

Turning his head, he looked at her through narrowed eyes, red-rimmed and wary. "Water...please."

Pouring a glass, she lifted his head. "Just a little."

He took a sip, but when she tried to pull the glass away, he gripped her wrist, holding it in place. After another few sips, he released his hold.

Her eyes lit with humor. "I can see you're going to be trouble, Mr. Eastman."

"Where am I?"

"You're in the Splendor clinic."

Joel tried to push up, then fell back, wincing at the sharp pain slicing through his head.

Rosemary placed her hands on his shoulders. "You must stay down."

"What happened?"

"A group of outlaws robbed the bank about the time you got off the stage. One of their bullets grazed your skull. Do you remember any of it?"

He started to shake his head, stopping when pain shot through him a second time. "Nothing. How long have I been here?"

"You were shot yesterday morning, so a full day."

A short knock sounded before Clay opened the door and walked inside.

"Doctor McCord. Our patient is awake."

Closing the door, Clay moved to the bed. "Mr. Eastman, I'm Doctor Clay McCord. How are you feeling?"

Joel lifted his hand, touching his head. "Like I've been run over by a train."

"The pain will pass in a few days. I can give you laudanum if it becomes too much." Clay checked the wound, then his pulse.

"No laudanum." Joel swung his legs over the side of the bed, trying once more to rise, his head spinning.

Clay reached out, bracing Joel's back when he began to sway. "It's too soon for you to be up and moving, Mr. Eastman."

Gripping the edge of the bed, he grimaced. "I've work to do."

Clay bent down and lifted Joel's legs while Rosemary steadied his shoulders, lowering him back onto the bed. "You're in pain, dizzy, and weak. Whatever work you have will have to wait."

Joel closed his eyes, resting his arm on his forehead. "I've been told to meet with Dutch McFarlin. Do you know him?"

"We do. In fact, Dutch was in here not long ago." Clay shook out the blanket, spreading it over Joel's legs and waist. "I must apologize, but we went through your clothes, looking for a way to identify you. When we found the Pinkerton badge and your trade card, I sought out Dutch. He's a former Pinkerton agent."

Joel didn't open his eyes. "That's what Allan told me."

"He's at the telegraph office now, sending a message to Mr. Pinkerton. If I know Dutch, he'll wait for an answer, then come straight back here."

Lifting his arm, Joel settled it on the bed, eyes opening to slits. "Good. I've business to discuss with him."

"Doctor, if you don't mind, I'll check on the other two patients."

"Thank you, Rosemary."

Joel shifted, his gaze following her out of the room. "You have a busy clinic, Doctor."

"We don't generally have three gunshot patients at one time."

"Three?" Joel choked out, covering his mouth when he started to cough.

"The gang who robbed the bank shot up the town, hitting you and two other men. Both are ranch hands at a spread south of town. One was shot in the leg, the other in the chest. He's the most critical."

"Did they catch the men?" Joel's voice lowered, his eyelids growing heavy.

"Not that I've heard. It was the second attack on the town by the same group. They killed a man when they robbed the bank the first time. We'd all just left church when they came storming into town. Everyone was there...Sheriff Evans, his deputies. The miscreants hit the bank and rode out." When Clay looked back at his face, Joel had drifted off to sleep.

The door opened a crack, Rosemary looking in. "Dutch McFarlin is downstairs, Doctor. He's asked to speak with Mr. Eastman."

Drawing the blanket under Joel's chin, he walked into the hall, closing the door. "It'll have to wait until after he wakes up again. Let Dutch know I'll send word as soon as Eastman is able to talk to him. By the way, did you hear anything about the outlaws being captured?"

Clasping her hands together, Rosemary shook her head. "The soldiers and Running Bear left the ranch before Dirk brought me to town this morning. Colonel McArthur believes the men who raided the town are deserters from Fort Connall."

"Are the Blackfoot helping to search?"

"No. They are returning to their village with Swift Bear. Wyatt said the soldiers are heading north to Wolf Creek Mountain to look for the deserters."

Clay's brows furrowed. "Isn't that the place some of the locals believe is haunted?" He and Rosemary walked down the hall to the room where one of the ranch hands recovered from his leg wound.

Her lips curved upward. "I'm certain those are rumors meant to keep white men away from the mountain. I mean, how could a spirit kill someone?"

"Good morning, Thomas. I'm here to see one of your guests." Travis shifted enough to glance into the Eagle's Nest. Several people sat in the restaurant, just not the man he hoped to see.

"Of course, Mr. Dixon. What is the name?"

"David Peeler." Travis noticed Thomas's nose scrunch at the name.

"He left a few minutes ago. I believe he mentioned speaking to Noah about renting a horse."

Travis felt pretty certain about where David planned to ride. "Thanks, Thomas."

Hurrying outside, he walked down the boardwalk toward the livery, nodding to a few people he recognized, not stopping to talk. Crossing the street, he spotted Noah and David outside, a large roan next to them.

"Good morning, Noah, David."

A grin spread across Noah's face. "Wyatt brought news the raiders are thought to be deserters from Fort Connall. He said the colonel and his men are riding to Wolf Creek Mountain. Seems a little farfetched to me, but…" He shrugged.

"Several of us feel the same, but it's the colonel's decision." Travis slid a hand down the horse's neck. "Are you going somewhere, Mr. Peeler?"

David's back straightened, his shoulders rigid. "Yes, I am, Mr. Dixon."

"Do you mind me asking where?"

"It's really none of your business." He turned back to Noah. "Now, Mr. Brandt, are we settled?"

Noah looked between the two, a spark of amusement in his eyes. "We are. Just be careful on your way out to see Isabella." He shot a knowing glance at Travis. "I sure wouldn't want anything to happen to you."

Glaring at him, David grabbed the reins. "I will most certainly be careful. Have a good day…gentlemen." Mounting, he reined the horse away from town, kicking it to get moving.

Travis let out a breath. He'd meant to speak with David about Isabella, come to terms with a possible union between them.

Noah crossed his arms, staring at David's back as he took the trail north. "I like that man less each time I see him."

"I know what you mean."

Clasping him on the back, Noah smiled. "Did you come here to talk to me or give Peeler a hard time?"

Chuckling, Travis turned his attention back to Noah. "A little of both."

Something had changed his thinking when he saw David again. He'd meant to discuss Arnott's request and David's ability to provide a good life for Isabella. Travis wanted to know if the man loved her or was pursuing her out of a sense of duty.

Each encounter with Peeler left Travis with a cold feeling in the pit of his stomach. Arrogant and self-absorbed, the man's actions and words did nothing to make Travis believe he'd be a good match for Isabella. She deserved much better than someone taking her on out of loyalty. Somehow, even that didn't sit well with Travis.

If Peeler had been loyal to Arnott, why had it taken him so long to make good on his promise? And why had he said nothing in all the letters he'd sent Isabella since her arrival in Splendor? Nothing added up to the man having the allegiance he professed.

Then a thought struck him. "Do you have a few minutes to talk?"

Noah looked at Suzanne's boardinghouse and restaurant across the street. "You know, I've had a yearning for some coffee and pie all morning."

"I like your way of thinking."

Noah took a sip of coffee to wash down the large bite of pie, his expression thoughtful. Setting down the cup, he crossed his arms.

"You're asking if I had trouble adjusting to marrying a woman with a substantial fortune. Is that because you're thinking of asking Isabella to marry you?"

Travis's mouth twisted a little. "I'm considering it."

"But you don't think you've anything to offer."

Sucking in a slow breath, he let it out. "I *know* I have nothing to offer. When you asked Abby to marry you, you already had a thriving business and a house on Sunrise Ridge. You had savings and prospects of your own." He snorted, shaking his head. "I live in a bunkhouse with the other men, train wild horses, and have about enough money to live on for two months if there's no work." He swallowed the growing doubt, feeling his chest squeeze. "Isabella would insist on us using her money." Meeting Noah's gaze, he shook his head. "A man can't live that way."

"A man can live any way he chooses. You're right about me having a business and a home.

They were nowhere near what Abby brought to the marriage. Back east, they'd call her an heiress. Out here, everyone knows she's a woman of means, the same as Caro and Lena. Both have enough of their own money."

"From what I've heard, Beau came into an inheritance."

Noah gave a quick nod to Beau when he entered the restaurant. "Not as much as Caro's worth, but yes, it was still significant."

"And Gabe is beyond wealthy with his hotel businesses back east." Travis massaged the back of his neck, afraid he'd never find an answer.

"You gentlemen mind if I join you?" Beau rested his hands on the back of a chair. He looked between the two, lifting his hands. "If you're having a private conversation, I can—"

Travis gestured to the chair. "Sit down. Noah's giving me advice and your name just came up."

Beau removed his hat, setting it on the windowsill. "Must be bad if my name was mentioned."

They waited while the server brought him a cup of coffee and took his order.

"Travis is thinking of asking Isabella to marry him."

Beau slapped him on the back. "Well, it's about damn time." Taking a hard look at Travis, seeing the green tinge to his skin, Beau's features stilled. "What's got your gut in knots?"

Noah held up his cup. "What do you suppose?"

Beau's brows drew together before his eyes widened. "Her money."

The sick feeling in Travis's stomach grew worse. "David Peeler came here to offer marriage. He's well-off and can take care of Isabella the way her late husband wanted. Maybe it's best if I step aside, let her be with someone closer to her station."

Beau leaned back in his chair. "Station? Do we even have those here in Splendor?"

Noah laughed. "Not so you could tell."

Travis gave them a disgruntled look. "You know what I'm saying. She has money, can live wherever she wants. Why stay out here in the middle of the frontier when she can return to a life of luxury in Pennsylvania?"

"It's simple. Isabella likes this town and loves you." Beau let the server set his plate down, picking up a fork. Stabbing a piece of chicken, he held it up. "Caro moved to San Francisco because she was so certain she preferred a big town, the theater, music, and a robust social life. Well, we all know what happened." Putting the chicken into his mouth, he chewed, a smug grin on his face.

"But you had a good job—"

"So do you."

"And you'd already bought a ranch," Travis continued, becoming more confused by the minute.

Beau glanced at Noah before giving Travis a hard look. "Does she want to marry Peeler?"

"She hasn't seemed too interested in his proposition."

Stirring a pinch of sugar into his coffee, Beau took a sip. "Can you live without her?"

Staring out the window at the bustle of wagons, horses, and pedestrians, he exhaled a slow breath. "If she chose him, I guess I'd have to."

Leaning forward, Beau rested his arms against the edge of the table. "Do you love her?"

"Of course I do. I wouldn't be thinking of marriage if I didn't."

Throwing up his hands, Beau stabbed another piece of chicken. "There's your answer. You love her, she loves you."

Noah chuckled. "I think what Beau's trying to say is to talk with Isabella, find out what she wants. If I know Dax and Luke, they'll build you a house on the ranch. Or they may offer to sell you some land...if that's what you want."

Crossing his arms, Travis's mouth drew into a slim line. "None of that solves the problem of her money."

Beau set down his fork, holding up a hand. "I think you're looking at this wrong."

Travis's brow lifted. "How's that?"

"Isabella's money isn't the problem. It's you figuring out if you're worthy enough to marry a woman as good as her. From what I've seen, you're the only man around who thinks you might be lacking. I can guarantee you Isabella doesn't feel the same." Reaching into his pocket, he pulled out a gold coin. "I'm betting if you ask her to marry you, she'll hesitate about a quarter of a second before saying yes." Slamming it onto the table, he sat back.

Staring at it, one corner of Travis's mouth lifted. Touching the coin with his fingers, he slid it back toward Beau. "I'm not taking your bet."

"Because you know I'm right." Picking up the gold piece, he slid it back into his pocket.

Noah drank the last bit of coffee, setting the cup down. "Isabella's not going to marry Peeler. If she had any intention of doing so, she'd already be on a stage with him, headed back to Philadelphia." Resting his arms on the table, he leaned forward. "Talk to Dax. Let him know your intentions."

Beau nodded. "Then ask that girl to marry you. Take it from me. It's the only way you're going to rid yourself of the misery you're in now."

281

Chapter Twenty-One

Isabella kept several feet between her horse and David's, wishing she'd told him no when he arrived at Luke's, asking her to accompany him on a ride. She'd said yes to spite Travis for leaving her without a word. Within minutes, the childish action had her miserable, wishing she could turn around and head back to Luke's.

Being around David was nothing like the comfortable, easy companionship she and Travis shared when they rode. Relaxed and self-assured, he made her feel safe, important in a way David never could.

His stiff frame bounced up and down in the saddle, forcing him to hold his hat with one hand, the reins in the other. If Isabella didn't feel so wretched, she would've laughed at the spectacle.

Coming to a fork in the trail, he stopped. "Which way?"

Shielding her eyes from the early afternoon sun, she briefly thought of directing him back to town.

"The trail on the right takes you back to Splendor. The one on the left takes us north for a ways before rounding back toward the ranch."

"Left it is." His confident voice didn't fool her.

Isabella knew David to be a man who avoided change and hated veering from his normal routine. She couldn't imagine how he'd made it from Philadelphia to Splendor without the help of his servants. The thought had her slowing Blossom, falling several paces behind David. She wondered why it hadn't occurred to her before.

Increasing her speed, she moved beside him. "David, why didn't anyone accompany you to Splendor?"

The question seemed to catch him unawares as he glanced at her before forcing his gaze back to the trail. "I decided to come alone."

"But you never used to travel alone. You always told me how much you hated going to New York or Baltimore. As I recall, you said if you didn't have at least one servant, you wouldn't go."

He looked at her, biting back the stab of irritation. "I no longer feel the same." David hoped the curt response would shut her up.

"It seems strange that after all this time you'd choose to come alone on a trip of over two thousand miles."

When he didn't respond, she continued to ponder his abrupt arrival, the odd letter he said was from Arnott, and his unapologetic demand they fulfill his friend's wishes.

She didn't remember him ever discussing marriage, except to say the institution wasn't for him. He preferred coming and going in his own time, not being burdened with the demands of a wife or family.

Arnott had once confided he believed David might not be attracted to women at all. Isabella remembered feeling confused until understanding had her mouth gaping open. Taking her hand, Arnott had squeezed it, reminding her not all men found women to their liking.

Her body tensed, wondering why she hadn't remembered Arnott's comments before now. Knowing his thoughts on David, she felt certain her late husband never would have discussed a possible marriage between them.

"David? Why have you never married? As I've thought about it, I don't recall you ever bringing a woman to the house or to any of the social events. I can't imagine a confirmed bachelor such as yourself wanting to be shackled with a woman at this time in your life."

His jaw tensed, his grip on the reins growing tighter. "My wishes aren't important."

"Of course they are. Arnott wouldn't have asked something of you he didn't believe would be of benefit to us both." She reined Blossom to within a foot of him. "What did he really ask of you, David? We both know it wasn't for us to marry."

Before he could answer, a shot sounded, their horses bucking. Isabella kept Blossom under control, watching in horror as David fell to the ground, smacking his head against a rock.

"David!"

Another shot rang out behind her. "Get off your horse."

The grizzled voice sent chills through her body. Looking around, she spotted a man limping toward her, gun raised. His hair appeared matted, clothes torn and dirty, as if he'd rolled around in mud. What caught her attention were his eyes. Dull, lifeless, showing no hint of humanity.

"I said get down." He spat the words out, raising the gun higher.

Heart pounding, she did as he asked, letting the reins drop. Her gaze moved to David. "We need to help him." She took one step, stopping when a bullet landed a foot away.

"*We* ain't got to do nothing." He limped closer, his eyes darting from her to the trail. "Give me whatever money and jewelry you have." Using the gun, he motioned toward David. "The same with him. I want whatever's in his pockets." When she hesitated, he fired into the air. "Now."

Hands trembling, she removed her necklace, thanking God she'd worn one that meant little to her. She'd brought no money or other adornments—except her simple wedding band.

Tossing the necklace at him, she knelt next to David.

"The ring, too."

Looking up, she shook her head. "No."

"You ain't in any position to bargain, lady. Take off the ring."

Isabella's hands stilled in the search of David's pockets. "You have the necklace and whatever is in his pockets. That's all you'll get from me." She knew being stubborn about a thin band of gold was ridiculous, but somehow, she couldn't let herself part with it. At least not in this fashion.

Feeling coins, she pulled them out, tossing them over her shoulder at their assailant while she continued checking pockets. Pulling out David's pocket watch, she stood, holding it out.

"That's all there is."

Taking it, he shoved it into a grimy pocket. "Now the ring."

Lifting her chin, she squared her shoulders. "I'll not give it to you. Take what you have and leave."

Her bravado waned for a moment when he took an unsteady step toward her, lifting the six-shooter to within a few inches of her forehead.

"I've already killed, lady. One more isn't going to matter."

She saw the instant his finger began to tighten on the trigger. Instinct controlled her as she turned her face to the side and lowered her shoulder, ramming into the man's chest. His wounded leg refused to save him as he tumbled backwards, the gun firing into the air.

For a moment, she stared, uncomprehending of what she'd done. Before she could think it through, she ran to him, smashing her foot onto the hand holding the gun, hearing a cry of pain. When his grip loosened, she kicked the gun away, anger seeping through her. She didn't stoop to pick up the weapon. Instead, she kicked him over and over, rage controlling her.

When solid arms wrapped around her, she screamed, continuing to kick into the air as she was lifted off her feet.

"Enough, Isabella."

Her arms flayed, trying to find purchase against the man holding her.

"Isabella! Stop."

This time, the voice cut through the anger, her breath coming in deep gasps, body going limp. "Travis?"

Turning her around, his worried gaze flew over her. "Are you all right?" A sound behind her had him pushing Isabella out of the way as he took aim. "Don't move an inch if you want to live."

The man fell back, hand holding his side where she'd kicked him. "Just keep her away from me," he moaned.

"David?"

Keeping the man in sight, Travis moved to Isabella, who knelt beside David. "Is he all right?"

"I don't know. He's breathing, but he has a deep gash on the back of his head." She looked up. "We need to get him to town."

"You." Travis walked toward the man. "Turn over onto your stomach."

"I ain't—"

Travis's foot pushed down on the man's bandaged leg, stopping his protest. "Turn over. Now."

Struggling, he gripped the ground, flipping over while Travis grabbed a rope from his saddlebag.

"Put your hands behind your back."

Using the rope, he tied the man's wrists, looping a length around his ankles. Ignoring the man's cries of pain, Travis drew his ankles up, securing them to his wrists. Lifting the man up, he draped him over the saddle of David's horse.

"You try anything stupid and I'll leave you out here." Travis holstered his gun, kneeling beside Isabella. "I'm going to get David onto Banjo's back."

Standing, she grabbed the horse's reins. "What do you want me to do?"

"Hold Banjo steady while I get David secured." Sliding his arms under David, he lifted. Getting him into the saddle wasn't easy. After a couple minutes, Travis swung up behind him, wrapping an arm around his waist. "Can you ride Blossom and hold the reins of David's horse?"

"I can." Another minute passed before Isabella mounted Blossom, gripping the reins of both horses. "I'm ready."

Travis sent a menacing glare at the outlaw. "You cause us any trouble and I won't hesitate to shoot you."

"Just don't let me fall off."

"Serve you right if you did," Travis muttered. "Let's go."

Splendor

"The Murtons brought one of their children in with a broken leg and another with a head injury." Rosemary looked at Travis. "They were playing in the barn when they were hurt. We had to move some patients around. Mr. Peeler will have to share a room with Mr. Eastman."

Travis groaned under the weight as he carried David up the stairs and down the hall. "Mr. Eastman?"

"One of the men shot during the bank robbery." She opened a door, indicating the empty bed next to Joel. "I'll do what I can until Doctor McCord can take a look. What about the other man you have, um...tied up?" The corners of her mouth slid upward.

"He's going straight to jail. I'll let Gabe figure out what to do with him. Isabella is going to wait downstairs for word on Peeler."

She bent over David, checking his pupils and pulse. "Let her know I'll come down as soon as the doctor knows anything."

Hurrying down the stairs, Travis spotted Isabella sitting in a corner of the crowded waiting room. "I'm going to the jail. Rosemary will be down as soon as they know more about David." He kissed her forehead. "Do not go anywhere without me." He placed a finger over her lips when she opened her mouth. "Not anywhere, Isabella."

"I *was* going to say I'll be waiting...and to hurry."

His eyes lit with humor. "Good." Walking to the door, he glanced over his shoulder. "This won't take long."

"He's such a nice man."

Isabella blinked, turning to face the elderly woman sitting next to her.

"Your husband, dear. So considerate. My Gerald was the same. You do all you can to keep him. Good men are quite hard to find, you know."

Although she'd heard all of what the woman said, her mind stuck on *your husband*. Isabella didn't correct her, enjoying the way the two words flowed through her. She did want Travis as her husband. What she didn't know was if he wanted her.

"Given the tattered uniform and boots, I'd say he's one of the deserters from Fort Connall." Gabe continued to study the man lying on a cot in one of the cells. "It'll be several days before we hear anything from Colonel McArthur. Until then, I'll learn as much as I can about our visitor."

"He was going to shoot Isabella, Gabe. Had the gun inches from her head." Travis ran a shaky hand through his hair, not realizing until this moment how scared he'd been when he saw the man holding a gun on his woman. If he hadn't already been on his way to Luke's and heard the shots, she might be lying on the trail right now. The thought sent an involuntary shiver through him.

"Whatever the man's done, he's going to pay, Travis. You can depend on it." Walking to the front, Gabe motioned to a chair. "Sit down."

"I need to get back to the clinic. Isabella is waiting to hear about David Peeler."

A grin touched Gabe's face. "Noah mentioned you're going to ask her to marry you."

Groaning, Travis lowered himself into the chair. "I'm thinking on it."

"If you do ask her, and she says yes, we have an empty house near the clinic. Wyatt and Nora live in the one next door. It needs a little work, but you're welcome to it if you have no other place to stay."

Straightening, Travis stared across the desk. "You don't have to do this, Gabe."

"I know that. I've got a house and you need one. It's yours until you figure out where you're going to live."

"I'll pay rent."

Gabe leaned back in his chair. "As I said, it needs work. You do the repairs and we'll call it even."

Standing, Travis reached his hand across the table, grasping Gabe's outstretched one. "Agreed."

"I'll take that to mean you *are* going to ask her to marry you."

Laughter rumbled through his chest. "I suppose I'll have to now that half the town has heard about it."

Standing, Gabe followed him to the door. "Yep. Living in a small town can sure change your life."

Chapter Twenty-Two

Isabella's gaze kept flickering to the stairs, her concern for David mounting as each minute passed without word. Recognizing the doubts she had about him and what she thought to be his true reason for coming to Splendor, she still didn't wish him harm. She wanted him to recover...and leave town.

The number of waiting patients thinned a little with Charles handling new arrivals and Clay taking care of the more urgent cases upstairs. When the front door creaked open, she glanced over, relieved to see Travis. Dutch entered behind him, both men coming toward her.

Standing, Isabella lowered her voice. "Did Gabe recognize the man who attacked us?"

Travis shook his head. "No, but he's pretty certain he was one of the deserters. With luck, he'll tell us what happened to the rest of the gang."

"And where to find them." Dutch's voice held a strong tinge of frustration. "Have you heard anything about Peeler?"

She clutched her hands in front of her. "Not a word."

"Doc McCord may not like it, but I need to speak with one of the other patients. The man with the head wound."

"Mr. Eastman?" Travis asked.

"That's right. Joel Eastman. He came to town to see me, but hasn't been awake long enough for us to speak."

"They ran out of rooms. Peeler and Eastman are sharing one at the top of the stairs to the left."

"Thanks, Travis. Let's hope Eastman is awake this time."

Isabella looked behind them at the two empty chairs. "I suppose all we can do is wait."

"Do you want to take a walk, get some fresh air?"

She thought a moment before shaking her head. "I wouldn't want Rosemary to come down looking for us and not know where we are."

Taking her hand, he threaded his fingers through hers. "I'll stay here if you want to step outside for a bit." He leaned toward her. "The air is getting stale in here."

Touching a hand to her forehead, she felt the sticky dampness. "You're right. I'll be—" She didn't finish, hearing the unmistakable sound of scuffling upstairs.

"What in the..." Travis's words faded as he dashed up the stairs, not noticing Isabella right behind him. Dutch's stern voice shot through the door of the room holding Eastman and Peeler.

"Settle down, Peeler, or I'll have to tie you to the bed."

"Let go of me. You've no right to keep me here."

Pushing the door open, Travis took in the sight before him. Joel sat on the edge of his bed, chest bare, head bandaged, a tight expression on his face. Dutch had David's arms pinned behind him. Looking at Joel, Dutch raised a brow.

"Are you sure this is the man you came for?"

"If he's David Peeler, then he's the right one. I've a warrant for his arrest."

Isabella gasped, her hand moving to cover her mouth.

"What's he done?" Travis slipped an arm around her shoulders.

"Stole a large amount of money from his partners. The charge is embezzlement." Joel spotted his coat hanging on a hook. "If you'll check my pocket, you'll find the warrant."

David blanched, his shaky voice pleading. "I've done nothing wrong, Isabella. You must help me." He struggled again, stopping at the feel of handcuffs locking his wrists behind him.

She stepped around Travis, walking up to Joel. "How do you know he's the man who stole the money?"

"I don't know all the proof they have on Mr. Peeler. What I do know is he left town in a hurry, missing a prearranged meeting with his partners. If you check his room, I'm certain you'll find a satchel containing a large amount of money."

She glanced between David and Joel. "Perhaps he needed the money for his trip west."

"His banker confirmed he is all but broke, and funds under his supervision are missing." Joel rolled his head, wincing at the pain before rubbing the back of his neck. "He'll get to plead his case in front of a jury. I can assure you, though, he's the right man. They have a good amount of proof."

Lips parting, she felt a mixture of contempt and relief. Everything fell into place for Isabella. David's urgency in coming to Splendor, why he wanted to marry her, and his insistence her late husband desired the union. She stepped in front of David.

"Arnott never mentioned us marrying, did he?"

Shoulders sagging, David appeared to shrink away, his face turning a pasty white. "No."

She stared at him, eyes wide with disbelief. "What happened to all your money? Your father left you a substantial sum, and your business always did well."

Shaking his head, he looked at the floor. "I lost it."

"Lost it?" Her voice rose. "How can you lose…" A vague memory appeared of an argument between Arnott and David. "You gambled it all away?"

"I didn't mean to, Isabella." He refused to lift his head to look at her. "The information I had was good, but nothing ever worked. I thought I could make it back on the next bet." His voice broke.

"But you never did."

"I tried, Isabella. Truly, I did. If my partners would've just let me use the money, I wouldn't have had to borrow it."

A red flush crept up her face, frustration and disappointment replacing her anger. "You *stole* their money, David. You didn't borrow anything."

"What is going on in here?" Clay stood next to Travis, arms crossed. "Mr. Peeler, you need to get back in bed." His eyes widened when he saw the handcuffs.

"Would you be able to treat Mr. Peeler at the jail, Doc?"

Clay pinched the bridge of his nose. "I'd prefer to lock him to the bed, Dutch. If all goes well, I'll release him to you in the morning."

Dutch unlocked the handcuffs. "Lie down and don't do anything stupid."

"I'm not a criminal," he shot back, but did what Dutch asked.

"The hell you aren't, Peeler. Embezzling money redefined your entire life. You'd best get used to it." Picking up David's left arm, he locked the handcuffs around his wrist and the bed frame, pulling to make sure it held. "May not be the most comfortable, but it's not the jail." Dutch looked at Joel. "I'll be happy to stay here tonight so you can sleep."

He touched the bandage around his head. "I may be a little dizzy, but I'm not incapacitated, McFarlin."

Dutch shrugged, turning back to Clay. "Send for me if there's trouble."

Clay moved to the side of the bed. "If you're all done here, I'd like to check Mr. Peeler's wound, then get back to the rest of the patients."

Isabella thought of saying more to David, changing her mind when Travis took hold of her arm. Walking down the stairs, her shoulders drooped. "I wish there was something I could say or do."

Reaching the first floor, he guided her outside. "David won't listen to a word you say, sweetheart. He doesn't believe he did anything wrong."

Dutch caught up with them, keeping pace as they walked between a couple buildings toward the main street. "Peeler will deny everything until he finally realizes the depth of the trouble he's in. I sure hope he can afford a decent attorney in Philadelphia."

"Is that where Mr. Eastman is taking him?" Isabella fidgeted with the fabric of her skirt, still trying to accept what happened.

"It is. I don't envy him the journey."

Stepping onto the boardwalk, they turned at someone shouting Travis's name. Dax and Luke reined their horses to a stop, expressions none too happy.

"Ginny's worried sick about you, Isabella. What are you doing in town?" Luke slid to the ground, tossing the reins over a post.

"I expected you back hours ago, Travis. We thought that group of deserters found you." Dax stepped up to him, his expression grim.

Travis rubbed his forehead, grimacing. "In a way, one of them did. Let's go into the jail and I'll explain everything."

"Have supper with me tonight, Isabella." Travis closed the door to the jail, leaving Dax, Luke, Dutch, and Gabe to further discuss the prisoner and the whereabouts of the other men. Not one believed they'd ridden to Wolf Creek

Mountain. He settled his arm over her shoulders, tugging her close. "We can go to the Eagle's Nest."

"I should probably get back and help Ginny. If I start now, I'll get there before dark."

Travis fingered the slim gold band in his pocket. He'd been fortunate to find it in Petermann's store before he left to find Isabella that morning. Never had he believed the day would turn out with David arrested and a member of the gang in jail. He shuddered each time the image of a gun, inches from Isabella's head, flashed in his mind. His arm involuntarily tightened around her.

"She'll be fine without you for another evening, sweetheart. I'll escort you back after supper."

Biting her lower lip, she thought of the few occasions they'd been alone. Most of their time together included other people—church, supper at Dax's or Luke's, the hunting trip. They deserved a few moments to themselves.

"All right. Would you mind if we went to Suzanne's?" The grin on his face told her she'd made the right decision.

"Wherever you want, sweetheart." He dropped his arm from around her shoulders, taking her hand as they continued down the boardwalk.

The late afternoon breeze felt good after so much time in the shared space of the clinic. Travis preferred being outside, working with his hands, seeing what he'd accomplished at the end of each day.

Opening the restaurant door, he stepped aside for her to enter.

"Isabella, Travis. What a nice surprise." Suzanne walked up, hugging both. "Are you here for supper?"

"We are." Isabella glanced at Travis before returning her attention to Suzanne. "And pie."

"Ah, so that's why you wanted to come here tonight." Travis settled a hand on the small of her back, following Suzanne into the dining room.

Isabella's face lit up. "Someone at the clinic said she made several fresh berry pies this morning."

"I did. How is this table?" Suzanne gestured to a table in the corner.

"Perfect." Travis pulled out a chair for Isabella.

"Would you like your pie before or after supper?"

"Both," they said in unison, then laughed.

Taking a seat, Travis leaned back, letting out a slow breath. "It's been a long day, Suzanne."

Glancing around, she decided to take a seat next to him. "I heard someone attacked Isabella and another man."

"David Peeler," Isabella said.

"Oh yes, the man you knew in Philadelphia." She patted Isabella's arm. "Well, you're safe and the outlaw is in jail. Where's Mr. Peeler?"

Travis chuckled. "Shackled to a bed in the clinic."

Suzanne's mouth opened, then closed. Standing, she shook her head. "You're going to have to tell me the entire story sometime. Right now, I'll get you some food. Pot roast is the special."

Both nodded.

"Pie first, pot roast second, and pie last, correct?"

The corners of Isabella's mouth tilted up. "Small slices for me, Suzanne."

"Big slices for me."

"I figured as much, Travis. I'll be right back."

Reaching under the table, he grabbed Isabella's hand and squeezed. "How are you doing?"

Enjoying the warmth of his hand in hers, she relaxed, her mind moving to the events of the day. "Tired, relieved, grateful I'm still here. If you hadn't come along..."

"But I did. You're safe, and I'm going to make sure you stay that way."

"What a nice thing to say, but not very practical given where we live. You're at the ranch and I'm at Luke's most of the time." Her eyes met his. "I'm not complaining. It's a fact. No one's completely safe out here."

Leaning toward her, Travis lowered his voice, glad for the privacy of their corner table. "We can get close to it, though."

Her eyes narrowed in confusion. "How?"

Reaching into his pocket, he pulled out the gold band, sending up a prayer he'd made the right decision. Pushing aside his fear and doubts, Travis placed it in the palm of his hand, holding it out.

"I love you, Isabella. Have for a long time. Marry me, sweetheart. Let me keep you safe."

When she just stared at the ring in his hand, saying nothing, fear began to build, causing a deep burn in his chest. Then her gaze lifted to his, tears filling her eyes.

She leaned toward him, cupping his face in her hands. "I love you so much, Travis. I'd be honored to be your wife."

Setting the ring on the table, he jumped up, lifting her into his arms. A shout of joy sprang from his lips as he twirled her around.

Laughing, she grasped his shoulders. "Travis, everyone is staring at us."

"And they should be." Setting her down, he turned around, his gaze locking on Suzanne, who stood a few feet away, a plate with pie in each hand. "Isabella just agreed to marry me."

A broad smile broke across her face. "Well, it's about time." Setting down the plates, she looked at the other diners. "This has been a long time coming. Pie is on the house tonight!"

Epilogue

A month later...

Reverend Paige closed his Bible, focusing his attention on the couple before him. "Travis and Isabella, you've carried the weight of many burdens alone. By the grace of God, you'll now share life's joy, pain, and pleasure with the person you love. I'm proud to have joined you in marriage. Travis, you may kiss your bride."

Whistles and cheers echoed against the stone walls of Solitude Gorge as Travis took Isabella into his arms, kissing her as if he'd never get enough. Raising his head, his heart raced, seeing the same joy he felt reflected in her eyes. Straightening, he took her hand.

"Ladies and gentlemen, may I present Mr. and Mrs. Travis Dixon."

Applause and congratulations greeted them as they walked amongst their friends. Glancing around, Travis couldn't imagine a better place to seal their future than in the spot where he'd spent so much time thinking of Isabella.

"She's a beautiful bride, Travis. Congratulations." Walter Evans shook the groom's hand.

"Thank you, sir. I don't deserve her."

Tilting his head back, Walter laughed. "None of us deserve the women who love us. By some miracle, they see past our faults and stand by us." He turned to walk away.

"I'm hoping for that, sir," Travis murmured, drawing in a deep breath, enjoying the scent of pine. Someday, he hoped to buy this land from Dax and Luke, build a house, and raise his own prime horses. For now, he felt content with a future he never thought possible a few short months ago.

"Here. It's time to celebrate." Wyatt held out a flask.

Travis didn't hesitate to take it from him. "Whiskey?"

"What else. I thought I'd share it with you before those two scalawags over there want to take a slug."

Travis touched the flask to his lips, following Wyatt's gaze to Beau and Cash. Taking a sip, he handed it back. "You can't trust anybody these days."

Wyatt shook his head, a grin curving the corners of his mouth. "Especially a couple lawmen."

"Have you ever been here before?" Beau asked Cash.

Taking a gulp of punch, he grimaced, shaking his head. "Never. It's a heck of a long ride for a wedding."

Looking across the field at Travis talking with Wyatt, Beau grinned. "Well, it took him a heck of long time to figure things out. I figure it's worth the ride to watch him make it legal."

"That it is."

Beau's expression sobered. "What do you think about the message Colonel McArthur sent?"

"You mean about finding a couple bodies a hundred yards up Wolf Creek Mountain?"

Beau nodded.

"The message said they weren't the deserters. I think the men who raided Splendor never rode north. They headed south. At least I hope they did. Gabe sent telegrams out to every town for five hundred miles. Someone's going to figure out who they are and get justice for those they killed. I just wish I could be there to see it." Cash's gaze moved to a spot several yards away, their voices carrying across the open space. "What's Mack doing over there?"

"Making a darn fool of himself." Beau took another sip of punch, choking on the syrupy sweetness.

"How many times has he asked Miss Lucero to supper and been turned down?"

"More times than I can count." Beau nodded toward Mack. "You can ask him yourself."

"Either of you have any whiskey?" Mack placed fisted hands on his hips.

Cash reached into a pocket. "I was saving this for a special occasion."

Mack didn't ask before grabbing it from his outstretched hand. Taking a long swallow, he shook his head, enjoying the slow burn. "Thanks, Cash."

"You look like you could use more."

"Nope. More than one and I might make a bigger fool of myself than I already have." He handed the flask back.

Beau sent Cash a knowing smirk, waiting for what would come next.

"Sylvia is the most stubborn woman I've ever met. Beautiful, willful, with a sweet smile and sharp tongue."

Cash glanced away to hide a grin.

"You have your pick of available women in Splendor, Mack. And you've made no secret of your desire to never marry. Why waste your time on the one woman who doesn't want anything to do with you?"

Looking at the ground, Mack shook his head. "Darned if I know." He looked up in time to see

Sylvia glance his way, gracing him with a coy smile.

"Don't fall for it. The woman's trying to tempt you."

"And succeeding," Mack ground out. "One of these days, I'm going to break down the walls Sylvia's built around herself and get her to say yes to having supper with me."

"Then what?" Beau asked.

Mack smirked. "I'm not sure, but I'll think of something."

Thank you for taking the time to read Solitude Gorge. If you enjoyed it, please consider telling your friends or posting a short review. Word of mouth is an author's best friend and much appreciated.

Watch for book eleven in the Redemption Mountain series, Rogue Rapids.

Please join my reader's group to be notified of my New Releases at: https://www.shirleendavies.com/contact-me.html

I care about quality, so if you find something in error, please contact me via email at shirleen@shirleendavies.com

About the Author

Shirleen Davies writes romance—historical and contemporary western romance with a touch of suspense. She is the best-selling author of the MacLarens of Fire Mountain Series, the MacLarens of Boundary Mountain Series, and the Redemption Mountain Series. Shirleen grew up in Southern California, attended Oregon State University, and has degrees from San Diego State University and the University of Maryland. Her passion is writing emotionally charged stories of flawed people who find redemption through love and acceptance. She lives with her husband in a beautiful town in northern Arizona. Between them, they have five adult sons who are their greatest achievements.

I love to hear from my readers!

Send me an email: shirleen@shirleendavies.com
Visit my Website: www.shirleendavies.com
Sign up to be notified of New Releases:
www.shirleendavies.com
Check out all of my Books:
www.shirleendavies.com/books.html
Comment on my Blog:
www.shirleendavies.com/blog.html
Follow me on Amazon:
http://www.amazon.com/author/shirleendavies

Follow my on BookBub:
https://www.bookbub.com/authors/shirleen-davies

Other ways to connect with me:

Facebook Author Page:
http://www.facebook.com/shirleendaviesauthor
Twitter: www.twitter.com/shirleendavies
Pinterest: http://pinterest.com/shirleendavies
Instagram:
https://www.instagram.com/shirleendavies_author/
Google Plus:
https://plus.google.com/+ShirleenDaviesAuthor

Books by Shirleen Davies
Historical Western Romance Series
MacLarens of Fire Mountain

Tougher than the Rest, Book One
Faster than the Rest, Book Two
Harder than the Rest, Book Three
Stronger than the Rest, Book Four
Deadlier than the Rest, Book Five
Wilder than the Rest, Book Six

Redemption Mountain

Redemption's Edge, Book One
Wildfire Creek, Book Two
Sunrise Ridge, Book Three
Dixie Moon, Book Four
Survivor Pass, Book Five
Promise Trail, Book Six
Deep River, Book Seven
Courage Canyon, Book Eight
Forsaken Falls, Book Nine
Solitude Gorge, Book Ten
Rogue Rapids, Book Eleven, Coming next in the series!

MacLarens of Boundary Mountain

Colin's Quest, Book One,
Brodie's Gamble, Book Two
Quinn's Honor, Book Three
Sam's Legacy, Book Four
Heather's Choice, Book Five
Nate's Destiny, Book Six
Blaine's Wager, Book Seven, Coming next in the series!

Contemporary Romance Series

MacLarens of Fire Mountain

Second Summer, Book One
Hard Landing, Book Two
One More Day, Book Three
All Your Nights, Book Four
Always Love You, Book Five
Hearts Don't Lie, Book Six
No Getting Over You, Book Seven
'Til the Sun Comes Up, Book Eight
Foolish Heart, Book Nine

Peregrine Bay

Reclaiming Love, Book One, A Novella
Our Kind of Love, Book Two

Burnt River

Shane's Burden, Book One by Peggy Henderson
Thorn's Journey, Book Two by Shirleen Davies
Aqua's Achilles, Book Three by Kate Cambridge
Ashley's Hope, Book Four by Amelia Adams
Harpur's Secret, Book Five by Kay P. Dawson
Mason's Rescue, Book Six by Peggy L. Henderson
Del's Choice, Book Seven by Shirleen Davies
Ivy's Search, Book Eight by Kate Cambridge
Phoebe's Fate, Book Nine by Amelia Adams
Brody's Shelter, Book Ten by Kay P. Dawson
Boone's Surrender, Book Eleven by Shirleen Davies
Watch for more books in the series!

The best way to stay in touch is to subscribe to my newsletter. Go to www.shirleendavies.com and subscribe in the box at the top of the right column that asks for your email. You'll be notified of new books before they are released, have chances to win great prizes, and receive other subscriber-only specials.

Find all of my books at:
https://www.shirleendavies.com/books.html

9 781941 786741